Dear America

The Diary of Angeline Reddy

Behind the Masks

SUSAN PATRON

SCHOLASTIC INC. • NEW YORK

For Richard Jackson,
with love

Library of Congress Cataloging-in-Publication Data

Patron, Susan.
Behind the masks : the diary of Angeline Reddy / Susan Patron. — 1st ed.
p. cm. — (Dear America)
Summary: In the "wild west" of an 1880s California gold-mining town,
Angeline investigates the supposed murder of her father, a famous criminal
lawyer, who she and her mother are certain is still alive. Includes historical
notes and instructions for making a mask from muslin.
ISBN 978-0-545-30437-5
[1. Frontier and pioneer life — California — Fiction. 2. Robbers and
outlaws — Fiction. 3. Diaries — Fiction. 4. Lawyers — Fiction. 5. Gold mines
and mining — Fiction. 6. California — History — 19th century — Fiction.
7. Mystery and detective stories.] I. Title.
PZ7.P27565Di 2012
[Fic] — dc23
2011023826

10 9 8 7 6 5 4 3 2 1   12 13 14 15 16

The text type was set in ITC Legacy Serif.
The display type was set in Rogers.
Book design by Kevin Callahan
Photo research by Amla Sanghvi

Printed in the U.S.A. 23
First edition, January 2012

Bodie, California

1880

Friday, June 4, 1880

Dear Diary,

I know I'm going to have to look in Papa's casket just to prove he's not in it. When we heard he got murdered, Momma took it pretty hard. I would have, too, if I'd believed it, which I did not. Stabbed in the back, the messenger said, on the stairway between Molinelli's Saloon and Papa's law office on the floor above. But Papa's much too smart to be dead.

This news was delivered tonight by a young clerk from the Wells Fargo & Co. office who said his name was Antoine Duval. He said "Madame" to Momma and "Miss Angeline" to me and explained that Wells Fargo was deeply saddened by our loss, which was also the town's. I think what he meant was that the town of Bodie would never have as great a lawyer — Papa had not once lost a case even though he often represented rogues and scoundrels that everyone else considered to be guilty. And he'd recovered a lot of the bank's loot stolen during stage robberies.

Mr. Duval regretted that the knife used by the

murderer had not been found and there were no other clues. Momma swayed a bit on her feet.

She had received him wearing a black veil to hide her inflamed cheek, caused by an infection from something lodged under her gum. Yesterday her cheek had swollen so much that it forced her eye to close.

Since she was in some distress, I took the paper Mr. Duval offered. "Look, Momma," I said to her, pointing to the signature.

She frowned at it. "This doctor must have been almighty liquored up or else on a choppy ocean when he declared my husband officially dead," she said, "since his name goes above and below the line and all the way off the page. Where was the doc when he signed it?"

"Molinelli's," Mr. Duval admitted. Everyone knew that of all the saloons in Bodie, Molinelli's had the cheapest drink, the crookedest gambling, and the worst brawls. Papa got a lot of clients just by going downstairs and offering his services when things got particularly loud.

"Well, I guess that's as good a place as any for

the doc to practice medicine," Momma said as she ripped the paper in two and threw the pieces over her shoulder. "But I believe he made a mistake about this particular death." When she gets mad, you don't want to be the person in front of her—she'll take it out on you for dead sure. I was glad that she had regained her spirits, but regretful that this young man was receiving the brunt of her fury. There are times when she embarrasses me nearly beyond toleration.

Since I didn't believe Papa to be in the least bit dead, I felt free to observe our visitor. Mr. Duval had ink stains on his long fingers, a thin white scar from his forehead down through his left eyebrow, and a rare gentlemanly grace about him. Dark hair curled at his neck, side whiskers shadowed his jaw, and a sharp Adam's apple jutted from his throat. His bearing was gallant and dashing. I imagined him as able to recite poetry while dancing a waltz, handle a dagger as well as a quill pen, strum a banjo or kill a rattler—what I mean is, he had the air of a man of numerous and dangerous talents—so he got my interest.

Antoine Duval bowed politely and tipped his Stetson to Momma. He turned to me and raised his handsome, tragic eyebrow. Then he did a most shocking thing that I confide here and only here in my secret diary. He winked at me, as if we were in a saloon and I were some sort of fancy woman. Yet it seemed more friendly than forward, and I returned his look with wide eyes and pink cheeks. As he backed out of the door, I wondered if the wink was a signal, not of any improper attitude toward me, but about Papa's supposed death.

Plenty of people had tried to kill Papa since he became a criminal lawyer. If someone finally succeeded, which is about as likely as church services in Molinelli's Saloon, I wanted proof of it.

Saturday, June 5, 1880
Dear Diary,

This morning Momma and I went to Dr. Rawbone's dental office as her infection was worse and she had developed a fever. The doc gave her a tincture of opium first, to lessen the pain. He said he would have to lance the boil on her upper gum — caused, he thought, by a bit of abrasive cuttle-fish in that awful store-bought tooth powder advertised in the newspaper. Momma, fierce and calm, sat in the reclining dental chair. Of course she insisted I observe and help — she had made sure I watched medical proceedings ever since I turned seven, and thus I had no fear of blood. I have seen bullets removed, knife wounds treated, toes amputated, bowels purged, and many babies birthed. I know nothing of the civilized parts of the world, but Momma says women out west need to be ready to do most anything, or someone is bound to die. Of course many die anyway.

I was given the job of holding a small gilded mirror in such a way that it reflected the light upon her face, for Dr. Rawbone's windows, none too clean, allowed scant daylight into the room. Each time he peered into her mouth, he commanded me to tilt the mirror to one side or the other.

At last he advanced and applied his sharp little tool. Immediately a great deal of blood, streaked with straw-colored pus, issued from her mouth, and filled the air with a nasty, fetid odor. The blood and pus ran onto a napkin tied around Momma's neck, and onto Dr. Rawbone's hands. He wiped his tool on his vest, took a breath, and gripped Momma's head, for she had lost consciousness. "Once more," he said, and again, blood and pus gushed out. I clutched the mirror, watching Dr. Rawbone, trying to breathe shallowly, as the stench was horrible. He seemed sure and quick, I'll give him that.

He pressed the gum with a whiskey-soaked handkerchief, wiping his tool again on his vest before returning it to the jumble of other picks and probes on a tray. Among the tools was a half-smoked cigar, which he lit. "Foul taste, pus. Swab it with whiskey." He seemed to be muttering to himself, but I paid attention in case he said something important. "Rinse. Warm salty water." He peered at me from around a cloud of smoke. "See to it. Three times a day." He frowned at Momma, then at me. "Get to the apothecary while she recovers. Buy laudanum. Buy a quantity. Be back here in half an hour."

I hurried down Main Street to the pharmacy, bought the medicine and a few penny candies, and with plenty of time left, nipped around behind Ward's Furniture and Undertaking Shop. Mr. Ward had a fine display of coffins, a rocking chair, and a curio cabinet in the front window, but I was interested in what was hidden in the back room.

No need to tiptoe, either. Carpenters hammered on three different buildings, a team of horses and mules pulled a wagon loaded with supplies toward the warehouse, and the stamp mill, of course, was pounding ore from the mines all day and all night. The racket from the mill was so loud and the force so great that it shook the ground. You could have screamed bloody murder and no one would have looked up from what they were doing.

Ward's back door, facing the alley, was ajar. I slipped inside.

I figured the big casket was Papa's because

someone, no doubt using the charred stick that lay upon the sawdust by my feet, had crudely written on its lid his initials, "PR" (for Patrick Reddy) followed by "Esq."

I lifted the lid. Papa wasn't inside. Though I hadn't believed him dead, relief washed through me, for here was proof.

There were also, judging from the weight when I hefted them, quite a few occupied coffins sized for small children and babies. These were grouped together to one side, and I didn't fancy staying long among them for fear their ghosts would try to seize me.

I looked around Mr. Ward's back room in the gloomy half-light. Five plaster death masks were lined up on a table, faces of men remarkably precise in every detail of wrinkle and hair, lip and lash. None looked familiar to me, even the one whose gray plaster skin was still wet when I touched it. The velvet curtain separating the front from the back room twitched a little, a sickly sweet smell rose up, and I figured it wasn't wise to linger amid the dead and their ghosts. It seemed a good idea to get away from there, as Mr. Ward would not take well to my sneaking into his establishment.

I grabbed the stick with its burned end and turned to go, wondering: If Papa was not dead, then where was he?

As I made my escape to the alley, I glanced back and saw the velvet curtain twitch once again. I think the undertaker may have seen me, for I got a glimpse of his sour face, but can't be sure.

I was peering through the road dust left by a passing wagon in the alley, about to retrace my steps to the dentist's, when a horrifying sight appeared from around the corner. A giant man with long rusty-colored hair and drooping mustache, as huge a human being as I've ever seen, lunged toward me, cradling a woman whose hands and dress were covered with blood. A small Chinese girl jogged behind him. As they came closer, I recognized the wounded woman and I screamed, for it was my mother.

I would have lashed that giant with my bit of blackened stick, except that my arms were suddenly caught from behind. I kicked backward like a startled horse, but my captor held me in a strong lock. There was a strange rushing noise in my ears, which eventually subsided enough for me to hear his voice saying, over and over, "She is all right, she is all right, she fainted but she'll be all right, we're taking her home."

At this, I went limp and he released me. I whirled around and before thinking I delivered a savage kick to his shin with my boot. He looked exceedingly pained and surprised but my satisfaction was short, for I finally noticed the scar running through his eyebrow: It was the handsome Wells Fargo clerk, Mr. Antoine Duval.

Furiously, for all of this was too much to take in at once, I turned back to the giant man, who had lurched on ahead carrying my mother in his arms as if she were a doll. "Wait!" I called. "What has happened?"

Mr. Duval was hopping on one foot, clutching his shin in both hands. "The dentist needed his chair for the next patient, so at his request we were TRYING to take your mother to her home," he said through clenched teeth. "He said she will recover PROVIDED she receives the proper care, which is exceedingly DOUBTFUL if YOU are to be in charge of administering it."

"Oh!" I said, and felt my face redden. "And may I ask what does any of this have to do with you?" At which he straightened up and looked at me levelly.

"I was having a private conversation with my acquaintance" — he nodded toward the giant — "in front of the dentist's office when Dr. Rawbone himself emerged and asked if I happened to know the patient and where she lived. I did, of course, as well as the dreadful situation of your father having been . . . having lost his . . . of your father's demise. So I offered to assist. We were ATTEMPTING to—"

"As my mother told you last night," I said, rudely cutting him off, "my father is not dead." Papa says I am as shy as a rabbit and he would have been shocked to hear my retort to Mr. Duval. I was almighty perturbed because I knew I'd be in trouble later for not returning to the dentist's office on time, with the result that Momma was now being carried through the streets by a stranger. That giant man strode back to us, easily supporting her as if she were a child, his massive forehead crumpled in worry.

"She wakes up for a minute, Antoine, and then she faints again," he said to the young man whose shin would have a large purple bruise on it tonight. "And her mouth bleeds still."

"Miss Angeline, you had better loosen her" — Antoine glanced at Momma's tiny waist and paused, for it would have been rude to say the word *corset* — "her . . . garment. I believe it is why she keeps fainting."

I knew he was right and I blushed. Momma had asked me to cinch the cords of her stays extra tight this morning. "Kindly turn your back," I barked at him.

He gave a deep theatrical bow and, turning, he murmured, "'Boldness is a mask for fear, however great,' as old Lucanus said." The words stuck in my frantic mind, for he was right — my boldness did mask my fear.

"You, sir," I said to the giant, "put her feet

on the ground and be good enough to hold her upright." It's true that I could never be as forward as Momma—some would call it unladylike—by commanding people to do my bidding, and it was scandalous for me to behave this way to grown men. The fear of losing her spurred me to unexpected impudence. To the Chinese girl I jerked my chin. "Do come over here and help me," I told her.

Though covered with road dust herself, the girl drew a spotless white linen from a cloth bag; she folded it into a small square and carefully lifted Momma's upper lip. Pressing the cloth to the bloody gum, she nodded at me. I frowned up at the giant man; he looked back at me like a soldier awaiting his command. I said, "Turn her so she's facing you and grip her by her arms—let her forehead rest against you—don't let her head flop back! And pray close your eyes." He obeyed me. In this way I was able to unbutton Momma's outer skirts and reach beneath to untie the corset laces and loosen them.

"All right, mister," I snapped to the huge

man, "now you can open your eyes and pick her up again."

At that moment, Mrs. Bessie Babcockry opened the back door of the wigmaker's shop, where she worked. Her hair, thick and golden, was arranged in artful disarray high on her head (in a way I have never been able to achieve, though I have tried mightily) like an advertisement for the small wiglets, curls, and false buns she fashioned. She flung a bucket of some foul liquid straight out in our path. When she saw us, she narrowed her eyes, dropped her bucket, and crossed her arms.

"Angeline Reddy, what the devil are you doing with them *men*? Taking a back alley like you got something to hide. The sight of your mother, passed out in broad daylight, would be shock enough for decent folks, and it's clear she consorted with them scoundrels — her underskirts are showing at this very moment — drinking spirits, frequenting opium dens" — here she glanced at the Chinese girl, who gazed back with a thin smile on her face — "and then she fell and bloodied herself. And dragging her only daughter along. A disgrace and a shame! Pray word of it does not spread, for it would stain the Reddy reputation, yet I'm certain others will want to know about this spectacle. . . ."

"Mrs. Babcockry," I began, so filled with fury I could barely speak. "Kindly do not—"

"Do not trouble yourself," Antoine Duval interrupted. "You must be exhausted, what with the huge pile of nuggets and bullion that Mr. Babcockry won at the faro table last night. I saw those winnings and I said to myself, *That man may have been a four-dollar-a-day miner this morning, which is a fine wage to be sure, but tonight he's the richest in town.*" Mrs. Babcockry and I both stared at him, at his earnest dark eyes and grave smile. Slowly, not taking her eyes off him, she turned her bucket upside down so that it formed a little seat. She sat on it.

"Excuse me," he said after a moment. "I am Antoine Duval, employee of Wells Fargo and Company. This is Mr. Monahan." The little Chinese girl seemed to have vanished.

Finally Mrs. Babcockry said, "What time?"

"Er, what time . . . what?"

"What time did my husband have all them winnings?"

"Ah! Yes. It would have been right around eight o'clock. That's when I said to myself, *If Mr. Babcockry gets up from the faro table right now, he'll walk out of here a rich man.* But I believe he may have ordered a round of whiskey for everyone, on the house, and I thought, *Well, he's a good sport to leave the boys with a glass in their hands.*"

Mrs. Babcockry got a hankie out of her pocket and used it to dab her eyes. Tears poured down her cheeks. "I didn't even know," she said, "that for a few minutes I was a rich woman and my sons had a wealthy father. By the time he got home, two hours later, he had not even two bits on him." Her rich, burnished hair framed a soggy, sad face and she looked as tired as if she hadn't slept in days.

"Let me give you a hand, Mrs. Babcockry," Antoine Duval said, and when she took his arm and staggered to her feet, he continued, "and if you'll give me yours, I'll put a small token of my esteem in it."

I watched as Mrs. Babcockry tentatively held out her open hand. With a flourish, he closed her fingers around a printed ticket.

"A special showing of the Horribles' latest play," Mr. Duval said. "It was given to me and I cannot be there, alas."

"Is it proper, though? I heard the Horribles is always in outlandish costumes, and telling tales out of school."

"The finest ladies attend," Mr. Duval assured her, "and the actors are paid richly by their laughter. The Horribles know everything about everyone in Bodie."

"Well," Mrs. Babcockry sniffed, "if them fine ladies go . . ." She patted a ringlet of her shining hair.

I glared, filled suddenly with a desire to throw a whole bucket of slop water on them both. Mrs. Babcockry may have fancied herself among the most proper of Bodie women, but here she was dallying with a stranger, and *he* was behaving in a sickening way, as courtly and elegant as a king. And all at Momma's expense, as she lay, semi-conscious, in Mr. Monahan's arms.

I said, "Thank you for your help, Mrs. Babcockry. We must be going. Good day." I turned to the men. "Come on," I ordered, and set off at a brisk walk, not looking back, kicking tin cans and trash in my way. Bessie Babcockry would spread the story so fast it would be all over town by the time we got home. She never understood Momma, who was not exactly like the other respectable ladies of Bodie. Ever since she married Papa, Momma had lived in mining towns like Cerro Gordo and Aurora and Bodie. She knew what it meant to be proper. And yet, she said, when pigs and chickens came into your kitchen because there wasn't any door at all, and only a dirt floor, well, that could make a woman see things a little different. It could make even a proper, respectable woman not pay the slightest heed to gossip.

Another burr under Mrs. Babcockry's saddle—she and everyone else knew that Papa loved Momma more than the moon, whereas most nights Mr. Babcockry fell asleep on a chair in a saloon. It was a place, he often said, that was more peaceful than his own home.

Mrs. Babcockry may have had the most beautiful hair of any man, woman, or child in Bodie, and she may have just received a most beguiling invitation to a Horribles play, but I wasn't going to waste one second giving a fig for her opinion.

Mr. Duval and Mr. Monahan left after depositing Momma on a chair in our parlor, and I was beginning to help her to her bedroom when the Chinese girl reappeared and supported Momma's other side, with startling strength for such a small girl. Glad for the help but surprised at her sudden appearance in our house, I wondered what new problem her presence could foretell.

"Who are you?" I asked when we had Momma settled on her bed. "Do you speak English?"

"Hush," Momma murmured. "Be more civil." Turning her head toward the girl with some effort,

Momma went on, "You are welcome in this . . ." and was suddenly asleep again.

"It's the laudanum makes her sleepy," the girl said. "Don't be giving her too much. Soon she'll crave it more and then more."

She was wearing a long, blue, threadbare jacket with loose sleeves, cotton trousers like a man's pajamas, and cloth slippers. A person could get dressed in one tick of the clock with clothes like that, instead of having an almighty number of buttons and petticoats and hooks and pins to do. Her hair was pulled back and caught in a long braid. It was shiny and straight. Mine was brown and flimsy and refused to be held in place by combs or hairpins, which fell out uselessly upon the floor. We both had unfortunate forehead wisps that were too paltry for bangs and too short to comb back. I wished I could trade clothes and hair with her, except for the forehead wisps, which I do not need any more of. "You don't sound Chinese," I said, meaning it as a question. She began removing Momma's shoes.

"Born in Bodie, not China," she said, and

I guessed that she'd had to explain this more than once. Most of the Chinese I'd heard in the Emporium or on the street were hard to understand because of their accents, but so were the Italians, Swedes, French, Dutch, and Indians. She asked, "Have you table scraps, an onion, some bones?"

"So you are a beggar," I said.

She put her hands on her hips and faced me. "Yes, beseeching the makings of soup for your mother. Well, I was, but not now. Not after you fixed on me begging 'em for myself." I flushed red. "Settle on if you want to trust me," she said, "even though I'm Chinese. Once you get it sorted out in your mind, let me know." She stared at me until I turned away, half shamed at my rudeness and half angry at her audacity. "Your father," she went on, and she scratched at a welt on her wrist, "didn't take so long as you are taking."

I whirled back around. "My father? What have you to do with him?"

"He helped us. Defended Sam Chung."

I'd saved the articles recounting the recent

23

trials of Sam Chung that ran in all our Bodie newspapers. Papa's ways of questioning and cross-examining witnesses made the spectators in the packed courtroom go wild, cheering and clapping as if he were Mr. William Shakespeare. He dug things out of people like a miner looking for gold, chipping and hammering away. No one expected Sam Chung to be acquitted of murdering a man whose mules ate his vegetables, but my father obtained a hung jury. The prosecution called for a retrial. Another hung jury. Finally, at the third trial, the jury unanimously acquitted Sam Chung.

Papa's successes made him a lot of enemies as well as friends. Suddenly I was plain worn out. I wanted Papa to come home, to take care of me and Momma. How weary I am of the recklessness and danger of Bodie! If only Papa would practice law in San Francisco, where not every man carries a gun in his pocket, and where there must be as many theaters and playhouses as we have saloons. I felt like a small child instead of a nearly grown woman of fourteen. The girl stood watching me. I asked, "How old are you?"

She shrugged, then said, "Nearly twelve."

I made a tell-that-to-the-jury face, learned from Papa, to show I didn't believe her. She looked barely ten. I went to check on Momma—she was still sleeping—and arranged some clean flour sacks around her head in case the gum were to bleed again. When I returned, the girl was gone. I stuck my head out the door and saw her neat small figure jogging toward Chinatown on King Street. "What's your name?" I called to her.

"Ling Loi Wing," she yelled back over her shoulder. As she disappeared around the corner, it occurred to me that I hadn't once thanked her.

I went in search of neck bones and other scraps of a cooked chicken, a potato, a bit of cabbage, an onion. I should be the real beggar, not Ling Loi, for I'd have begged to take back my unwelcoming ways. Regret was the bitter ingredient in the soup I finally made.

Monday, June 7, 1880

Dear Diary,

This morning Momma awoke feeling better but she is not a good patient—she is much too *impatient*! She and Papa long ago decided I should become a nurse, following in Momma's footsteps, but I am as unsuited for nursing as she is at being nursed. Of course I care for her diligently, but in truth I'd rather do most anything else.

She wanted to dress and attend to the work of the house, but I had already scrubbed the kitchen floor, cleaned the chimney lamps, and made biscuits for supper. I begged her to rest and to rinse her mouth with warm salted water as the dentist urged, and she finally agreed that she would. She insisted I go to school as usual. Soon she was once again sleeping, her wound still raw and tender.

I am forced to attend school even though most likely by now I know as much as the teacher. Before leaving, I went to Papa's little antechamber, his home office, where he keeps notes on his legal clients—figuring I may find some clue about his disappearance. My father has escaped serious injury and death over and over, and I had heard so many stories of his dangerous livelihood, defending accused thieves and murderers, that I almost didn't believe he could ever die.

I was shocked to find the door to his antechamber locked, as I'd never noticed it *had* a lock — even the front door to our house does not have one, as I believe only banks and shops have locks in Bodie. I had read the words on the bronze plaque affixed to Papa's door a hundred times before, but today they struck me like a secret passcode.

Truth, Enter Freely,
Be Witnessed,
Find Justice.

Something about the silence beyond the door drew me, as if Truth were an actual being within. If Momma were better I'd ask her about this, or perhaps try to find the key myself.

School is always a torture, and how much

better educated I would be if I were allowed to remain at home reading books on my own. (I have already read *Little Women* by Louisa May Alcott many times, and *Ragged Dick* by Horatio Alger, and the plays of Wm. Shakespeare, and Papa's copy of *Walden* — these are the books, plus of course Momma's housekeeping book and the Bible, that have traveled with us each time we moved.) Yet my ideas about self-education are not understood by my parents, however often I explain them. My mother also longs for me to have religious instruction, but as we have no church in Bodie I am safe for now, and in any case I have read the entire Bible twice. There is a saying among the miners that once a town has either a church or a hanging, it is time to move out. So far, we have had neither and there are only streams of folks moving *in*.

Teacher Minnie Williams had taken a dislike for me on the first day, for what reason I do not know. It may be because her brother, Con, is rumored to be a member of the secret citizens' committee of vigilantes, called the 601. These citizens believe the law is not always as swift or as just as it should be, and at times they have forcibly driven out of town, in the middle of the night, certain persons *they* judge to be guilty of law-breaking. This has happened even after a jury declared the person not guilty. My father often spoke out against the vigilantes.

News of Papa's supposed death had spread through town, and Miss Williams was clearly shocked to see me. She made me come to the head of the classroom while she questioned me in front of the other students. I have always felt that she would have done better to work in the mines, for she had the determination of a mule and the strength of two men. I do not know if bossiness is a needed quality in a miner, but she had that, too.

"Why are you not in mourning?" she demanded, as I was wearing my usual calico dress instead of black clothing required of the bereaved. She was older than Moses but all of us scholars knew how strong she was, and we tried not to make her raise her voice because it could pierce your eardrums with its sharpness.

"Because I do not mourn my father," I answered.

"What insolence and ill-breeding," she screeched. "Your father raised a crude and ungrateful daughter, going against God and nature." In this way, she insulted both Papa for being a poor father and me for failing to pretend grief.

"But, mistress," I said as politely as possible under the circumstances, "would you have me lament someone who is not dead?"

Miss Williams looked aghast. "His death is reported in both the *Daily Bodie Standard* and the *Daily Free Press*, Angeline Reddy," she said in a harder tone, the one to which we have been taught never to answer back. "Who are you to contradict two newspapers as well as your teacher?"

I stared at the floor, knowing I should not reply unless to agree.

One of the Babcockry boys, the older one, Hank, spoke out from the back row. His voice was changing, so mostly it was deep but every so often it jumped, going up high, just to remind him, I suppose, that he's not a man quite yet. He said,

"My pa tole me everyone knows Mr. Patrick Reddy was a one-armed Irish shyster." His voice slid up on *one-armed* and made him sound like a sick cow until it went back down again on *Irish*. Papa had lost one of his arms in a gunfight before I was born, and thus met Momma, who was his nurse. She convinced him to become a lawyer. He has been called a shyster before, meaning *dishonorable*, although surely it's because people are jealous of his great and unmatched skills in defending the most guilty-seeming accused. Then Eleanor Tucker, who is older than me by a year and has a constant stream of beaus *and* a rich daddy, said, "Miss Williams, may we please return to our geography?"

Eleanor is most studious, and I confide to you, dear diary, that this can be an almighty irritating aspect of her. She seemed to be implying that geography was more important than Papa, but it was Hank's worse insult that made me forget proper behavior when standing before the classroom.

"And yet my Papa can do more with one arm

and his smart brain," I retorted to Hank, "than your father could do with two of both."

Miss Williams stamped her foot; I felt it through the floor like when the mills are pounding ore from the mines. She said, "Hank Babcockry, go stand in the cloakroom until I say you may come out. While you are in there, think about unruliness in this classroom, talking without permission, and speaking ill of the dead." He shuffled to his feet, the tallest boy in the class and also the skinniest. As usual, he wore an old pair of his father's pants, too big around the waist and held up with a rope.

Miss Williams continued, "Ellie Tucker, stand in the corner and balance your geography text on your head as a reminder of polite behavior." Then she turned back to me. "Angeline Reddy, hold out your hands." I'd never had my hands paddled, though I'd seen the welts they raised on the hands of others.

One of the smallest children in the front row began to cry very quietly, the Higgins sisters clutched each other, and both the towheaded

Fouke boys looked down at their desks. No matter how much we fought among ourselves, none of us liked to see another get the paddle. Glancing up, I caught a sympathetic look from Eleanor as she rose from her seat.

The paddle was kept in sight on Teacher's desk, a reminder to us students. Miss Williams seized it and smacked it, ferociously, onto my outstretched palms and fingers. At once my hands felt as if they had been thrust into a very hot fire; they throbbed and stung and the pain got worse, then worse still. Tears came to my eyes and all I could do was to hold my hands before me as if they were frozen in that position. I did not cry out.

"Be seated, Angeline," Miss Williams said.

I stood there, bent over, gasping, and it was difficult to hear, while the tears in my eyes prevented me from seeing. It was as if my other senses had closed down and there was only searing pain.

One of the Higgins girls in the front row, Beverly-Ann, tugged at my skirts. She tugged and tugged, and dimly I realized that Miss Williams was still holding the paddle and looking at me through narrowed eyes. She insists that her students receive punishment stoically, without showing any emotion. I turned finally, straightened, and walked to my seat. I kept my throbbing palms and fingers from touching any surface for a good long while.

All afternoon I could scarcely hold my pencil with my thick and useless hands. The welts matched the pattern on the cane paddle.

At home I was not much help to Momma. Though I tried wrapping my hands with flour sacks, I could not carry the heavy buckets of water needed to wash the blood off her clothes. Momma was not herself, being weepy and agitated over Papa, who should have sent a message to us by then. Finally I told her about sneaking into Mr. Ward's establishment by the back door and discovering that Papa's casket was empty. She rallied at this news and I was thankful that she ignored my boldness as a trespasser along with my failure to return to Dr. Rawbone's office in time. She is more than ever sure that Papa lives. Many times before, during trials and investigations, he has disappeared or been called away, so we are confident that he is working on a case.

I gathered up the soiled cloths, leaving her to doze, and on my way to the lean-to cellar, I made a discovery. The girl, Ling Loi, was standing just inside of our door.

"Message for you," she said. She did not smile.

"Yes?"

She waited. I frowned. I could wait as long as she could. But what was this game we were at? How could she be so gentle and kind to Momma, yet to me behave like an outdoor cat that has never known human touch?

Finally too exasperated for this to go on, I said, "Well, what are you waiting for?"

"Your answer."

I thought back to our conversation, yet could recall no question or request. I got the last of the bread pudding out of the pie safe and put it in the center of the table with two spoons. She flicked a glance at it, then gazed at the wallpaper. She scratched the inside of her forearm.

I picked up one of the spoons and put it into her hand. She set it back on the table.

I sat down and placed my hands on the table, palms up so she could see the marks on them. "I had my hands paddled today," I said, "because I talked back to the teacher. I told her my father wasn't dead, even though the newspapers said he was. Now tell me: Is your message from my father?"

"I still wait to find out if you trust me," she said. "I'm as Chinese today as I was Saturday. Yes or no." Then she added, "Also I was educated in a brothel and I sometimes work for criminals."

I fanned myself with an old copy of the *Daily Free Press*. Polite people are not supposed to mention brothels, although it is a fact that there are dozens of these places where women entertain men on Bonanza Street near Chinatown. I would love to catch a glimpse of those women, for I have heard that they tell bawdy jokes and make themselves beautiful by painting their faces with emulsions and powders and by wearing gowns with low necklines, but they stay indoors and I am not even permitted to go to Bonanza Street.

Everyone always says Bodie is the wildest and worst of all the mining towns, but *I* never get to see much more than the regular saloons on Main Street, and that is just the same all the time — tired, dirty miners and cardsharps passing money and whiskey across the tables and shooting their guns — usually, but not always, at the ceiling.

"I'd enjoy seeing a brothel, but I do not want to know anything about your work with criminals," I remarked, to show her she couldn't shock me even though she just had. She said nothing. I must summon the faith of Peter to be able to hold up even a shred of a conversation with her. I asked, "Do you not want bread pudding?"

She shook her head. We were both wearing exactly what we'd been wearing the other day. Her bony, flea-bitten wrist looked as fragile as a teacup. It made me feel distressed.

"My mother is recovering," I said. "I thank you for your help."

She nodded once.

I remembered that Momma says we should

be kind to everyone we meet, as we are all fighting a hard battle.

"Please sit with me at this table. We can play a game of cards or I'll read to you." She continued to stand where she was, a person with no amusement in her, as if laughter were a special skill that has to be learned, and no one had bothered to teach her. After another minute she turned toward the door.

"Wait," I said. "Ling Loi, please wait. I'm sorry. I'm . . . tired and my hands hurt and I'm scared about Papa."

"I know that," she said. She reached for the knob of the door.

"And I do trust you."

She turned and pinned me with her eyes. It felt like being in the sights of a very steady rifle. She said, "*Even though* I'm Chinese?"

I flushed, for she mocked my difficulty in trusting what is unknown and unfamiliar. I felt like one of those old ladies who act scared of everything, and it was not a way I wanted to be. "Yes, *even though* you're Chinese."

"Then how old am I?"

That made me smile because it was a test I could pass. "All right. You look as if you are ten but you told me you are nearly twelve. So you *are* nearly twelve. I believe you. I trust you. Now will you give me the message?"

She opened the drawstring bag hanging from one wrist, the same bag that had contained the clean cloth for Momma's wound. She reached inside for something and drew out her closed fist, extending it to me. I knew she was daring me to open my own hand to receive whatever it was. My palm was tender still, and I had no idea what would land in it, but all of a sudden I *did* trust her. I reached out and caught the small metal object she dropped. Then she was gone, out the door, leaving me no chance to ask further questions. But I knew I held one of the answers.

Papa's message to me lay in my hand: a key.

Tuesday, June 8, 1880
Dear Diary,

It is a great relief that Papa is not dead, even though his funeral will be soon. Momma and I will not attend it, nor will we wear mourning clothes today. Momma fails to realize that this may cost me another paddling, as I determined not to tell her about yesterday's punishment. She is weakened and has worries enough.

Nor have I told her that the key brought by Ling Loi matched the keyhole to Papa's antechamber and that early this morning I went in. Papa's papers were all of a jumble on his desk, and I figured if Truth were there, discovering it would be an almighty task. I felt again a waiting presence, as well as a scent like running water, a stream. My nerves were much disturbed as there was no such stream nearby.

What could Papa have wanted me to find? Why had he led me here? I made to sit at the desk and, pulling back his chair, discovered a large envelope on the seat. I stared, not touching it at first, for in a bold, unembellished hand was the number "601." Somehow Papa was caught up with the secret vigilantes, the men who took the law into their own hands, and *my* hands were loath to occupy themselves with anything of theirs. Finally I reached for it, turning the envelope over to find it sealed with red wax. An image had been engraved on the seal and pressed into the wax—it was a mask, symbolizing, I think, the stealth and secrecy of those men. For a moment it made my flesh crawl. I returned the envelope to Papa's seat and pushed in the chair.

The tension in that room was like a stick of dynamite. I knew I should wait and allow whatever truth it was to find me, yet I feared that knowing the truth would be like lighting the dynamite's fuse.

I left without disturbing any of Papa's papers. Later I will try to decide what to do to help him.

At school I gave a hard candy to Beverly-Ann as thanks for tugging my dress yesterday, for she pulled me out of the maze of pain and kept me from further reprimand.

Miss Williams made no mention of my calico dress, though she shunned me as if I were not there. I wondered if she herself had ever felt the effects of the paddle. If she had, I doubt she would ever use it to discipline a student again.

As we all left the schoolhouse in the afternoon, Eleanor Tucker came to me privately and commiserated about the paddling and Hank's insulting words. Always before I had no mind to speak to her, as she makes me impatient with her string of beaus and the perfect curls on her forehead and her womanly curves — for I have singed bangs that no amount of time with the curling iron will make pretty, the shapeless shape of a boy, and no beaus. But she pressed upon me the gift of a special salve and it soothed my hands wonderfully. She said she would never have spoken out if she'd known it would end with the paddle and she begged me to forgive her.

So we have become a little more friendly than before, and thus one good thing came out of that terrible day.

I returned home to find Momma slightly improved.

Mrs. Babcockry arrived with a covered basket, plenty of words of sympathy, and barely concealed hopes for new gossip. I wasn't overly worried that Hank had told her about my getting my hands paddled, for it would have meant revealing his own disgraceful role in that event.

"Bessie," Momma said, without inviting her in. "We're obliged for the basket but have no need of condolences, for Mr. Reddy is not dead."

"But, my dear," Mrs. Babcockry said hesitantly — she was a little wary of Momma's temper, having encountered it before — "his murder is a well-known fact, Lord have mercy."

I saw tiny lines I'd never noticed before on Momma's forehead, and dark smudges under her eyes. Ordinarily she would have set Mrs. Babcockry right straight, but now there was resignation and weariness on her face. The look she gave me seemed like a plea for help. I stepped up beside her on the porch, blocking the entrance to prevent our visitor from pushing her way inside.

"Yes," I said, as if in agreement with Mrs. Babcockry. "We, too, have seen the newspaper accounts of his murder. And I'm certain Papa's in a better place now." Mrs. B. seemed relieved. It simply would not do for Papa's wife and daughter to spoil the funeral and the wake by disagreeing with known facts.

But for an instant, Momma's lips had twitched; she knew I was neither lying nor telling the whole truth, either. In this way I am sometimes a bit like Papa. An artist can make your eye look at a canvas and see not little green dots on top of a blue smudge, not paint at all, but leaves and a patch of sky. That is how Papa uses words.

Mrs. Babcockry was inching forward, so I asked, "Do you recall if any of the stories mentioned whether my father was going upstairs or downstairs when the stabbing occurred in Molinelli's? It seems like the answer could provide a . . . clue, don't you agree?"

I tried to figure how Mrs. Babcockry fashioned her curls so as to wave handsomely in different directions; it seemed to me unfair that some people have magnificent thick locks while others such as I must make do with mere thin scraps for hair. She peered around us for a look into the parlor. "I *did* read some mention of that," she said, "at least I *think* I did, and if not, someone should ask Sheriff Kelley about it. I had better see to it right away."

"Thank you so much, Mrs. Babcockry," Momma said. "You're very kind, and now forgive me for I must rest."

At last Mrs. Babcockry stopped trying to edge her way inside; I guess she was in a hurry to find the sheriff and question him. She beamed at Momma and me and patted a perfect ringlet, looking well pleased with her visit.

I hoped that the basket she brought had in it something good to eat.

Wednesday, June 9, 1880

Dear Diary,

Tonight I longed again for Papa, for I felt frightened and unprotected. When we heard the vigilante mob whooping and rampaging through the streets, Momma made me clean and oil the revolver and the old rifle Papa keeps in a wooden box. We knew that, whatever the mob's goal or destination, it was safer to stay indoors and hidden. I hope not to shoot as I hate the pounding recoil, I hate the deafening noise, and I hate the smell of gunpowder. Papa shakes his head when I protest each time he bids me practice. He says I will not hate remaining alive when some other is bound on killing me.

Momma said they have no reason to want to harm us, and I should not be afraid. But I think reason is not what governs these vigilantes. There is some other thing, some powerful thing, and part of that is hiding behind a mask. The mob would not go against the law so boldly if their true identities were known.

I went around closing curtains as Momma took her bottle of medicine and retired to bed. I stood in the parlor, feeling as if the house had grown bigger, or I smaller. There was a sound in front like the tap of a shoe heel on our wooden porch. When no knock on the door followed, my stomach lurched a little. I picked up the revolver and stared at the door. Still no knock; nor any other sound. My apprehension grew; I could not endure not knowing who was outside. My courage was thin as a thread, but the strong rope of curiosity lassoed me and pulled. I decided I would rather find out than stand there quaking all night.

I turned low the wicks of the lamps. Slowly I inched the door open and slipped outside, closing it behind me. A moth fluttered against my face, someone coughed, and I nearly shot my foot off.

"Who's there?" I hissed. Speaking in a normal voice seemed ill-advised for some reason.

"Excuse me. Antoine Duval." I could see him off to the side, in the moon-shadow of the house. He, too, spoke in a low voice. "May we go inside?"

"No," I said rudely. "What do you want? Why do you creep around our house?"

"I'm . . . conducting a search. Not a search, exactly, but an examination. Of the houses along this street."

"And to what end are you conducting this

examination?" He had this way about him, now as before, that seemed partly interesting and mysterious, but partly devious as well, and I suspected he was lying.

"Miss Reddy, it's not safe out here. The vigilantes are liquored up and wild. I'm trying to keep track of their whereabouts."

"Maybe you should just listen for a lot of whooping, and keep a sharp eye out for hooded men riding fast."

He laughed softly. "You sound like Swift."

"Who?"

"An Irish satirist, as are you. But you must go in, a better choice than the place he called 'Where fierce indignation can no longer injure the heart.'"

I was interested in that. "What place did Swift mean?"

"Death," he said. "Swift wrote his own epitaph. Now go inside and write some mocking words of your own on another theme. I admire your tone."

"Well, I do not admire yours. I have much work and no time for fanciful writing." This lie was my own, for while it is true I have little time, there is always, dear diary, some of it left for writing.

"Shhh," he whispered. Something made me clamp my retort in my teeth, though I wanted to launch it at him like a spitball (a particular art I last practiced at the age of eight). Then I heard an approaching horse. "It's one rider, not the mob," he whispered. "Go inside and I'll stay hidden nearby to keep watch. If they come in a mob I'm going to have to try to trick them."

I stayed where I was. Mr. Duval was not to think he could order me about. I guess I have some of Momma's bit of temper, the kind that turns its back on good sense. She says our angry stubbornness makes the two of us real good at cleaning every bit of grit out of a corner, but poor at hasty decisions.

Moments later a hooded horseman rode straight to the porch. He must not have seen me, for he yelled over his shoulder, "This here's the Reddy house! Over here!"

His voice slid up an octave on *house*. I said, "What are you doing, Hank? Does your mother know you're riding around with a hood on your head?"

His horse had scented me, but Hank must have had an almighty shock to learn I was standing there in the dark — and that I knew him. He jerked back on the reins with one hand while adjusting his hood with the other. I realized I could see him much more clearly than he could see me, and that flour sack with eyeholes in it wasn't helping him. In a deeper voice he said, "Git down off that porch and come over here."

"Why?" I said, full of the knowledge that Antoine was listening. I guess I was showing off a little, pretending more bravery than I had. Besides, it was only Hank, in his daddy's too-big-for-him trousers. "I live here. I'm holding my revolver I just cleaned and I sure hate to fire it, especially with my hands still a little sore. But I can fire it and I'm a good aim. You know the best way to aim, right? You just act like the gun's your finger that you're pointing straight at the target. Did you come to murder my papa again?"

"I ain't never murdered him the first time."

"That what you want your tombstone to say?"

I still had the words of Swift in my mind and fierce indignation in my heart.

"Tole you to git down here." Another rider appeared to the left of the house, the opposite side from where I'd seen Antoine. I hadn't heard his horse on the softer ground as he walked it slowly around from behind. He carried a flaming torch and gave a low whistle as he guided his horse next to Hank's.

I said, "Friend of yours, Hank?"

The new arrival muttered, "How she know who you are?"

I laughed and said, "I recognize your voice, too, Con Williams." He was Teacher's young brother. In spite of my bold act, I was beginning to worry about the situation getting rough.

He ignored me and said, "This the house we burn down?"

I turned cold all over. My hands shook like a miner's after a night in the saloons — I could barely hold the revolver, much less fire it. My water threatened to rush out of me uncontrollably like an infant's.

I wondered when Mr. Duval would make his presence known. Then many things happened quickly and nearly all at once.

Con Williams lifted his sidearm in my direction. I heard a shot and expected to be dead. Con swore and dropped his flaming torch.

The door behind me was wrenched open and a rifle was fired over my shoulder. I became deaf for many moments from the explosion near my ear.

Hank fell off his mare, which immediately bolted, raising dust as it followed the other retreating horse.

Momma jerked me inside, slamming the door. I peeked out the window at Hank, who seemed to have lost the rope holding up his trousers, for he was hopping around in his drawers. I dashed out back to the outhouse, where I relieved myself in time, then hurriedly returned to the parlor.

A knock, followed immediately by the door being opened by Mr. Duval, his hands high in the air. "Mrs. Reddy," he said. "Was anyone hit? Are you both all right?"

She aimed the rifle in his direction.

"We are unharmed," I said hurriedly. "Momma, it's that Mr. Duval from the bank. He was covering us."

She ignored this information and the possibility of being civil.

With the rifle still aimed at him, Momma said to me, "Angeline Maude Sullivan Reddy, what the devil were you doing out on the porch knowing those thugs were about? I'm ashamed you carry the names of everyone I love best in the world." She meant her sister, her mother, Papa, and, I guess, myself. She was trembling, though whether from fear or anger I cannot say. Carefully I placed my hand on her arm; carefully I lowered the barrel of the rifle. Carefully, carefully, I pried her fingers off the stock.

"They're gone, Mrs. Reddy. Your daughter faced up to them." He advanced slowly, looking (I noticed) almost more Irish than an Irishman, as Frenchmen sometimes do — those that have long narrow noses and thin lips and curly black hair. "They won't come back, but I'll stay nearby, to be sure."

Some great pent-up force seemed to go out of Momma. She sagged, and I caught her before she crumpled. Mr. Duval helped her to a chair. I went to the kitchen for water.

When I returned, he was gone. Peering through the window I saw him scraping sand with the side of his boot over the last flames of the burning torch. I watched as he looked around. He seemed to be listening. After a while he merged into the darkness and I turned to attend to the weapons and, worse, to face Momma.

Tea and Mrs. Babcockry's meat pie calmed her down some. She explained that she hadn't taken her medicine after all, since it made her sleep too deeply, and glad she was that she hadn't, or we'd both probably be dead right now.

"But Mr. Duval fired at them just when you did, Momma," I began. There was a tap at the door. "That's him now," I said. "He said he'd be back."

I ran to open it, but it wasn't Antoine Duval. It was Hank Babcockry, hoodless, grasping a wad of trouser cloth at his skinny waist.

"Come to ax you something," he said.

I glared at him. "Where's your gun, Hank?" I said.

"Give it up to that Frenchman Duval and another fella—he kept in the shadows and didn't talk much—couldn't say who he was. And I tole them where I heard the mob is heading and promised Con and me won't do this no more, so they let me go. I lost my rope," he finished in a mournful way. I waited. Worse things had happened this night. Momma spoke up.

"Oh, for pity's sake, let him come in, Angeline." I was not too surprised. Momma had always had a soft spot for Hank, and I lost track of how many times over the past two years that he sat in our kitchen getting broken bones splinted and wounds patched up. When I was younger I was even a little jealous of how much she babied him. "Hank, you better not have that other delinquent with you," Momma added.

"No, mam," he said. "I ain't."

I moved back slightly to allow him to pass, closed the door, and waited by the table where I'd set the revolver. I crossed my arms. Last year I saw

Hank kiss Ellie during the game of grace hoops. Now he was scaring women in their homes.

"What is it you want?" I finally asked. I noticed he'd ripped his shirt and scraped his cheek; he was lucky it wasn't worse. He smelled like it was a little past time for his weekly bath. I knew he kept away from home as much as he could, for his father was mean when he drank. His eyes slid to the tray that still contained half of one of his mother's meat pies.

Momma said in a weary voice, "It is late, Hank. Eat the rest of that pie Bessie made and tell us what you have to say."

Hank's hand shot out. He crammed the food into his mouth as if he were starving. Momma and I exchanged a glance; she'd seen it, too, something worse than bad manners. I believe he *was* starving. I went once again for water. Pausing at the stairs, I dashed up and got something from Papa's bureau. Downstairs in the kitchen I put it in a clean lard pail with two apples, biscuits, and some jerky. Papa says hunger and poor treatment are as bad for a boy as for any animal. When I returned, Hank was standing in the same spot. He burped.

"Didn't your mother give you any of her meat pies?" Momma was asking.

"Yes, mam, but my father wouldn't let me have much. He says I got to earn my keep in the mines. Guess I'll start that soon as I can get hired." He looked at the carpet for so long that I looked, too, wondering if there was a bug of some sort that had distracted him. There wasn't. Finally he said, "I am right sorry we scared you. I want to ax you please don't tell my pa about it. That's all."

"You mixed up with the 601, Hank?" Momma talked gently, so he'd know he could answer without flaring up her temper.

He said, "No! Mr. Tucker said we couldn't—I mean we was just coming over on our own, like a joke, but people started shooting and it waren't turned out like we planned."

"A joke!" I said. "You and that Con Williams ride in here with rifles and torches and call it a joke? You insult my papa in school and expect us to—" I broke off, remembering too late I hadn't intended to let Momma know about that and the paddling.

"I thought on that. I oughtn' a said what I did about your daddy."

Momma stood. "Hank, you are thirteen years old and you have done a stupid thing. I'm ashamed of you; you betrayed this family and me. If you raise a gun, someone will shoot you. How can you not know that?" Her voice was strange, like she had a sadness-sickness. "Playing at vigilantes. It's a miracle that you are alive. Now go." She turned away and left us, Hank looking stricken.

How is it possible to feel such extreme fury and such numbing pity for the same person at the same time? I had no words, but maybe Momma's disappointment in him was enough. I shoved the lard pail into his free hand and pushed him out the door.

Thursday, June 10, 1880
Dear Diary,

Last night I was too tired to continue writing, for Momma and I stayed up late after Hank left. I learned something I'd always wondered about but never known.

She patted the side of the bed when I passed her door, her hair loose, both of us in nightshirts buttoned to the neck against the evening cold.

"Did you take your medicine finally, Momma?"

"No. You know, Angie, there's a quantity of opium in it. I was starting to want it like a prospector wants whiskey, and that's bad. Should have realized sooner."

"Well, take a little if your gum hurts."

"I'm all right. Are you?"

I was going to say "yes, mam" but didn't. I wasn't.

She asked, "What did Hank say about your father in school?"

"Called him a one-armed shyster. Is he? A shyster, I mean?"

She hesitated. "Well, Patrick goes by the law. Some of his clients have had rough lives and he loves to help the underdog. You have to understand that some of the accused that go free — it's not necessarily because they're innocent, but because the jury couldn't agree and find them guilty. There's a difference."

"So he helps guilty people go free?"

"People are innocent in the eyes of the law until *proven* guilty. And sometimes they don't go free — they have to go through another trial with a different jury."

I thought about that. After a while I said, "Mr. Duval and that 'other fella' outside let Hank go tonight."

"Hank was a fool and worse to come here and almost get someone killed. But he's still just an overgrown boy been treated bad by his father for years. Maybe kindness, or one more chance, makes more sense than punishment. I don't know for sure." She pulled her shawl around her shoulders. "You went upstairs. What did you give him in that lard bucket besides food?" she asked.

"Papa's old leather belt," I admitted.

She nodded. "He should not have to be humbled on account of his clothes."

"Shall I get you another blanket, Momma?"

She shook her head and waited, eyebrows

raised. She knew very well I had more thoughts churning around inside.

"The gunfight," I said finally, "the one when Papa lost his arm before I was born. The two of you always talk about how you fell in love during the time afterward when you nursed him and got him to give up gunfighting and study law."

"Now you want to know how it happened," she said.

"I have asked before, but no one would talk about it."

"Even I probably don't know the whole story. Maybe your father doesn't, either." She paused and then I knew she was going to tell me. "He and your uncle Ned were partners in those days, following new gold discoveries and living in mining camps. This was in Aurora during its boom. One day they were hunting in a canyon near town and another hunter saw movement and fired a shot that hit Patrick in the arm. Mistook him for game."

"So it was just an awful accident."

"Well, more like an accidental gunfight. Instead of revealing himself, the man stayed hidden. So Ned fired back — the only time he ever missed — and then the man threw out his gun and began bellowing and crying. He was sore afraid and ashamed. Ned said he was the worst sort of coward and vowed he would even the score in a fair fight, once Pat got seen to by a doctor.

"But the man helped Ned carry Patrick to town. Later he paid all the doctor bills. He was real sorry he acted like he did. And your father convinced his brother to call it quits — no more bloodshed. In time we found out the shooter was known as a confidence man around the mining districts. He started to accumulate money and bought shares in successful mines. People liked him because he was a natural leader, and he was generous. He organized volunteer fire departments in the camps and planned games and balls for holidays. A few years ago the man and his family moved here to Bodie."

"The man who shot Papa lives here?" I could not figure this out. Why hadn't I ever heard about it before?

"I used to try to befriend his wife, but she

always seemed reticent and kept to herself. They have a daughter, and this is another reason why Papa and I have not told you the story. The girl doesn't know, and I doubt the wife knows. The man asked us, for their sake, to keep it quiet — he says he's ashamed even though it was an accident. I also suspect he fears retribution from your father's friends if they knew about it. We decided to forget the past and get on with our lives. This man does not speak of it; nor do we. And nor, Angeline, must you."

Something made me wish I hadn't pressed Momma to reveal these old secrets. I did not want to know more, but of course at the same time, I *had* to know more. "Who is it, Momma?"

When I was little, Papa would sit me between them on the bed. I would cross my arms, giving one hand to Momma and one to him. Right hand to Papa's left, left hand to Momma's right. They would match my fingertips one by one to theirs, reciting "pinky, ring finger, middle man, index, thumb" and then Papa would kiss the tip of my nose and say he had all the hands he needed.

Now Momma took my left hand and silently touched each of her fingertips to mine. She said, "I'm telling you now because I don't trust him. I believe he's dishonest. I want you to be careful." And then she looked at me and said the name of a rich, well-liked leader in Bodie, one of its prominent citizens.

Darryl Tucker.

My new friend Eleanor's father.

I took this knowledge to bed, along with the revolver. We were not bothered again, though we heard shouting and whooping throughout the night. A metal gun barrel is a cold and sorrowful thing to sleep beside.

Friday, June 11, 1880
Dear Diary,

This morning, as I stood barefoot in my old nightshirt waiting for water to boil, sorting the mending into piles of urgent, very urgent, and most urgent, I heard a tap at the back door. I was lazy from sleeplessness and hadn't dressed.

Thankfully, it was Ling Loi, but she was not alone. A large, drowsy puppy was draped in her arms, appearing as heavy as a little pig.

She looked at me, then at the dog. "It belonged to the Walheims," she began.

"Who?"

"The family the vigilantes forced out of town," she said.

"Do you mean Mr. Walheim the boot maker over on west Main?" The puppy lifted its head and yawned. I yawned, and then Ling Loi yawned. It is the most curious thing that a dog can send a yawn to a person and then every other person will catch it, too.

"Yes, the cobbler, his wife, and a bunch of children, some of 'em almost grown. The vigilantes killed this dog's mother, who was trying to defend the house."

"Well, that's an almighty shame. What crime did they say Mr. Walheim committed to get kicked out of town?"

Ling Loi shrugged. "Two weeks ago there was a fight at the Parole Saloon. No one knows who started it, but when the deputies got there Mr. Walheim had a pistol in his hand so they arrested him. He was out on bail waiting for the trial but his lawyer . . . got killed." Her face showed no sign of any opinion about this, though of course she knew he was alive.

"My father was his lawyer?"

She shifted the puppy's position so that its head hung over her shoulder. The dog was a sound sleeper. It had brown hair and big ears, just like me. "That's what people are saying. They claim the vigilantes didn't want to wait until Mr. Walheim found a new lawyer; they didn't want to wait for a trial, so they decided he was guilty and ran the whole family out of town. That's all I know, except this dog needs a home."

"Not here, Ling Loi. I have no time for a puppy and dogs make Momma sneeze. You keep it."

"I cannot. I have no . . . place for it."

I shrugged and poured hot water into a basin for Momma. After she washed, I'd take it out and pour it on the vegetable seedlings, though there was little hope of them surviving. There is not a single tree here, or for miles around — the only plants are stringy, prickly desert shrubs and wild grasses. It is hard for most things to grow here, in a place 8,000 feet high. "Well, give it to a boy. Boys always want a dog."

"No. I will not. Boys are mean."

"Ling Loi, I'm almighty busy." Almost as soon as I said it, she was out the door. I went after her. "Hold on. I have an idea. Let me get dressed and take this to Momma. Wait on me for a minute."

I dashed to Momma's room with the water, spilling some on my nightshirt, but excited with my new plan.

Now it is late and I must go to bed, so tired I can hardly keep my eyes open to write, but tomorrow I must tell what occurred when Ling Loi and I left the house with that puppy dog, for it is a surprising story.

Saturday, June 12, 1880
Dear Diary,

"We are going to call on Mr. Johl," I explained to Ling Loi as we walked toward Main Street yesterday. "Do you know him?"

She shook her head and the two slim feathers of her eyebrows drew together in a frown. She looked not at me but at the dog and said, "I'll wait for you outside."

"Oh, he's a nice man. Momma buys our meat from him and says he gives large cuts for a fair price. Perhaps he and Mrs. Johl could use a dog to guard the shop at night. Please try not to scratch at your flea bites while we are there or they will think it is flea-ridden."

She looked at me. "Oh," she said in a sarcastic way. "Maybe *you* should carry the dog to keep it from getting my fleas."

"I did not mean that. But why do you have fleas?"

"I haven't fleas. I have flea *bites*. From my customers, the inmates at the jail. They give me their bedding and clothes to wash, and, oh, the fleas.

Hard to kill—you have to smash them with the back of your thumbnail, or drown them if you can." We were keeping to the edge of the road, for it was thronged with miners carrying their empty food pails, finished with their all-night shifts, heading for home or the saloons. "The prisoners pay me in gold dust or coins. Some of them are too poor to pay. If I like them I do their clothes *pro bono publico*. That means 'for the public good.' I do it for free."

I knew what it meant because Papa takes a lot of *pro bono* legal cases, which Momma says is why we are not rich. "It must be horrible, the jail."

"I have friends there. We call it the Hotel de Kirgan because Constable Kirgan runs it, the boss man. I have to bribe him with a portion of my pay."

She was a surprising girl. "But your parents do not worry? They allow you to do this?" Mine would not even let me walk along Bonanza Street, at the end of which was the jail.

She made a clicking noise with her tongue. "No more questions." The dog began to squirm and she put it down on the dirt, where it immediately began to sniff. I kept walking. I did not have time to chase puppies or worry about girls. A miner shoved Ling Loi and aimed a kick at the dog, which she snatched up just in time, keeping beyond his reach. He cursed at her.

"Hurry up," I said to her. "Let's get this done."

But then in the midst of all this commotion — weary, filthy men going home; new families arriving in town on wagons and on foot; shopkeepers hurrying to open their shops on Main Street — right then a voice I knew well screeched my name. It was Miss Williams, her sharp elbows assuring plenty of leeway among the other travelers. The miners kept well out of her path.

With a sinking heart I greeted her, continuing on my way, but she bid me wait.

"Angeline Reddy," she said. "I believe the school is in the other direction."

"Yes, Miss Williams," I said, trying to look as

innocent as possible, since I *was* innocent. "I shall not be late, just running a little errand before the bell rings."

"No doubt," she answered. "And who is this?"

"Nobody. Just a girl, Miss Williams."

"Name?"

"Ling Loi." Ling Loi glared at me and then turned to Miss Williams with a look of terrible fear. She inched nearer to me. I believe she was too afraid to run.

"I have heard about you, Ling Loi Wing," Miss Williams said, a horrifying pronouncement. No one ever wants to be the subject of something Miss Williams has heard about. "It was the Presbyterian Mission Home in San Francisco, a Miss Culbertson, who contacted me. Someone had written to her with a most improbable story of a Chinese girl living in squalor here in Bodie. Of course there are hundreds of Chinese here, but *you*"—she leaned forward, as if to see Ling Loi at the closest possible range—"are the *only* Chinese *child* that I have seen." Miss Williams stopped speaking and fixed us with her piercing eyes. She waited.

When Ling Loi did not respond, Miss Williams said, slowly and quite loudly, as if Ling Loi were deaf, "What is the dog's name?"

"We do not know, Miss Williams," I said. Of course, I then realized how foolish I was being, for Miss Williams did not care what the answer was, only whether Ling Loi understood her.

Then Miss Williams did a strange and unexpected thing. She reached out one of her bony hands for the dog to sniff. It licked her fingers. Ling Loi smiled. Miss Williams petted one silky ear. Ling Loi smiled more.

Miss Williams drew herself up, her head tilted back, and looked down at me fiercely. "Well, Angeline, is she?"

I racked my brain but could not figure out what Miss Williams wanted to know. This kind of situation, of not understanding the question, could be almighty bad. "Is she what, Miss Williams?"

"Living in squalor, Angeline. What do you think we are talking about?"

I had *thought* we were talking about the dog, but I saw that Miss Williams moved like a knight in the game of chess — in two different directions. I glanced at Ling Loi, who had a sweet expression on her face that was new to me. She looked fragile and tender, and I could tell by the way she tilted her face prettily that she had had to wear that mask before, to cover up her scowl. At the same time, she reached one arm behind us, still cradling the dog in her other, and pinched me.

I looked straight back at my teacher. "Of course not, Miss Williams. What I mean is, of course she is not living in squalor." *Squalor*, whatever it was, did not sound good. But even if she were living in it, I figured Ling Loi did not want to be rescued by the Presbyterian Mission Home.

"We shall see," Miss Williams said. "And Angeline, do *not* bring the dog into my classroom."

With great relief we finally parted ways with Miss Williams and hurried on toward Mr. Johl's butcher shop. I hoped to find, not only a home for the dog, but some pigs' feet, which can be boiled a long while and then packed with their bones in a stone jar with cider vinegar. This is useful to have on hand in the larder, as it keeps well. Momma pulls off some of the meat and stirs it with a thickening of flour and water to make a nice breakfast souse.

Thinking of pigs' feet made me hungry and I paused to look at the slate menu outside the Occidental Hotel and Restaurant. "Mmmm," Ling Loi said, "they have fresh oysters."

I hadn't supposed she could read English, and was surprised. How had she learned that? Even more surprising, she had tasted fresh oysters, a costly dish here, far from the ocean. I asked her how it came to be that she'd eaten them.

"Oh, I have had everything on that menu, partridge and veal cutlets with truffles, and ice cream and champagne besides," she said.

I decided not to show her for one second how preposterous this sounded to me. Should a person doubt Ling Loi's word, it is best not to let her know it. "How grand," I said in a neutral way. "And who taught you to read?"

She shrugged as if it were obvious, and answered, "Same people who gave me the food."

I peered through the window at ornate chandeliers, velvet-backed chairs, gilded mirrors. "I bet this is what it must be like in San Francisco," I remarked. "Fancy restaurants and shows —"

"I would hate to live in that Home in San Francisco," Ling Loi interrupted. "They probably give you some kind of soupy gruel and hard bread. I'd run away if they made me go there."

"Would you run away to China? Would you stow away on a boat?"

"Never," she said. "Well, not never. Someday when I am very rich and have many servants and sons. If I went to China now, I would only get sold to some man as *mui jai.*"

"What's that?"

"Indentured servant. Like a slave. And he'd ship me back here to Gold Mountain anyway, to work off my debt. At least for right now I can do work I want and keep the money."

"'At least for right now'?" I repeated.

But Ling Loi pointed to a sign on the door that made us stare at each other after we read it.

NO SCRIP ACCEPTED. U.S. CURRENCY ONLY.

"That does not make sense," I said. "Scrip is the only money the miners have — it's what they get paid for their work! Everybody uses it!" I knew Ling Loi had seen plenty of scrip, too — like gold dust or nuggets, it was more common than regular U.S. currency. Papa was always paid in scrip when he defended miners, and other people, too. Not that we ever dined at such a fancy restaurant as the Occidental.

The dog stretched out its nose every time someone walked past us, as if it had to sniff everything in the world. Ling Loi shifted it to her other shoulder. "Will that teacher try to make me go away?" she asked.

I shrugged. "You were cute with her. I think she liked you."

"I know."

I made no comment on Ling Loi's modesty or lack of it. But in fact she was just being honest. As we walked, she explained.

"When I was a little tiny girl," she said, "miners paid to kiss me. They had not seen a baby in a long while, I suppose, and never a Chinese one. One miner paid an ounce of gold to hold me for an hour so he could smell me and kiss my face. It is true!"

"Ugh," I said.

"I did not mind it," she said, "*then*. But if it was now, ugh."

I laughed. "Lucky for you. You were like a little gold mine with none of the work."

I was surprised when she scowled at me. "You do not understand, Angie. You could never understand."

We had arrived at Mr. Johl's shop. Ling Loi seemed reluctant to go inside, but I opened the door and pushed her in.

It was still early, but the day was warming

and Mr. Johl's big bald head gleamed with sweat. Behind him some carcasses hung. He wiped his cleaver on his apron and leaned forward on his palms, peering at us over the huge worktable. "Ha! No bones for dogs until end of the day," he said. "Come back later."

"I want to buy some pigs' feet, sir, if you have them," I said, "and we were hoping you needed a good strong dog. No fleas." I shot a sideways look at Ling Loi to remind her not to scratch.

He seemed to inspect the dog and Ling Loi both. He laughed. "That is a pup, not a dog."

"This pup here is a smart one, Mr. Johl. Its mother was the bravest dog in Bodie."

"Maybe," he said, and went back to work, rending a mighty blow to a joint on his table. "I will ask Mrs. Johl. It is possible." He nodded to us. "Pick up your pigs' feet when you return. Pay in dollars—no scrip."

"But, Mr. Johl, I have only scrip. My mother, Emma Reddy, is too ill to go to the bank today."

"Ah," he said, and looked anew at me. "Of course, of course, you are Miss Reddy. Bring your scrip, then, and we will make do."

"Thank you," I said, wondering how we would manage, if all the shopkeepers began not accepting scrip. Wondering how anyone except the very rich would survive.

We started to leave when Mr. Johl came around from his table, reaching for the dog. Ling Loi gave it to him, and it seemed to all but disappear in his huge hands. "Ha! Leave the dog," he said. "We will see."

Later

I hurried on to school, not wanting to be late after that encounter with Miss Williams. Ling Loi headed toward Chinatown.

A handbill that had been much trampled upon caught my eye at the edge of the sidewalk, for written large across the top was HORRIBLES WANTED. I have inserted it here:

HORRIBLES WANTED
Famous Acting Troupe Reveals
Skeletons in Closets for
ENJOYMENT
of All
If You Like the Stage, Join the Horribles and
Skewer the Rich and Famous of Bodie Townsite

ALL IN FUN!
Beginning and Advanced Thespians May Apply
Expect Not Much Money but Ample Delight
Major Performance Scheduled for
Fourth of July Celebration

Rehearsals 6 P.M. Every Tuesday Henceforward,
Courtesy of the Occidental Hotel
Ask at Hotel Desk for Mr. Horrible

NOTE: Script-Writers of Plays and Skits about the
AUTHENTIC LIFE
of a Western Mining Town May Also Apply

*Sponsored by the Occidental Hotel and Restaurant
and by the Committee of Arrangements for the
Fourth of July Ball and Parade*

Of course, dear diary, you know I could never go up on a stage and perform, as my tongue would turn to stone, my teeth would lock shut, and I should die of fright and embarrassment. In any case, I believe it rare for women to become Horribles. However, how I would love to write the lines for the actors to say! How I would delight in knowing all the players' identities, and in passing freely among them, going backstage and providing what help I could in the production. Since finding the notice, I've done nothing so much as dream of becoming a member. It is said they are so excellent that one day they will take to the road, performing at theaters in all the great cities. Oh, how grand it would be to join them! Inside my mind, I envisioned a play about the

AUTHENTIC LIFE
of a Western Mining Town

and I began to hear the actors' voices. I started to know what they would say, and the terrible and comical things that would befall them.

Perhaps I should invent my pen name, against

the day when I become nearly as famous as Mr. William Shakespeare. Like the Horrible actors, I shall mask my true identity.

After school, as I headed for Main Street, worrying about Papa, an idea came to me. It seemed at first too bold, too much of a risk, but my feet made the decision to detour toward Fuller Street, where there is not a saloon, not a hotel, not a business, nor much of the usual traffic of animals, carts, and wagons — only cabins and houses.

I know this street because back in February, during the hardest winter anyone recalls, when many died from the cold and consumption and dreadful fevers, and a dozen children were taken by diphtheria, Momma and I made our way here on snowshoes, pulling a little sled through huge drifts of snow. People called it the "pneumonia winter."

We brought supplies and food to the houses where no smoke came from the chimneys, for in them were the untended sick and the dying, with no one able to keep a fire going. It was along this street where we had heard a faint weeping from within a large fine house. We stopped at the front door. The face of my classmate—beautiful, studious Eleanor Tucker—appeared at a window and then she had let the curtain drop, nor opened the door, so we went on our way. Momma said people's sadnesses are their own concern, and that respect for their privacy is the most charitable gift.

Today I found Eleanor outside, whacking a braided rug with a carpet beater that made me cringe inwardly, so much did it resemble Miss Williams's paddle. She nodded on seeing me and made to go inside, but I called to her.

"Eleanor, wait," I said. "I need your help. Will you give it?"

She glanced at the house, dropped the carpet beater, and hurried to meet me, a finger to her lips. Grabbing my arm, she pulled me back the way I had come. All of this encouraged me in my enterprise.

When we were some distance, still walking rapidly, I said, "I have heard that the Walheims were driven from town by the 601." I kept to myself our encounter with Hank Babcockry and Con Williams. "Someone" — I didn't say that it was Hank — "mentioned your father. Is he a member of the citizens' vigilantes? Do you admire them?"

If she was surprised at these direct questions, she didn't show it. "No, I do *not* admire them. Before, I thought they were keeping the town clean. There was just too much lawlessness for the sheriff and the constable and the few deputies to handle. But hounding whole families out of town — those poor Walheims!" After a moment she said, "You asked about my father. Did you know he is a great philanthropist? He helps so many people, and he helps the town, too. Right now he's working with other volunteers on all the games and contests for the Fourth of July celebration."

I frowned at her. Too much bragging, I thought, about a man with secrets: the secret of the accidental shooting, and maybe the secret of his being with the vigilantes. I had to risk my new friendship with Eleanor by asking, "So since he's the Patron Saint of Bodie he wouldn't have been part of that vigilante group . . . ?"

Her eyes grew wide and she stopped walking. I feared she would turn and stride away. "Angeline," she said, "I don't know. My father . . . is complicated. Mostly he is calm and jovial and kind — pulling coins out of boys' ears and giving peppermints to little girls. And he loves me fiercely. I know he would give his life for me. But" — she touched my arm lightly — "may I speak frankly, trusting that my words will be between us alone?"

I nodded. "I promise."

She continued, "I confess to you that there is another side to him. A side I do not understand. Sometimes he has outbreaks of rage. He'll say to my mother, 'You made us lose hope!' and then she'll cry and go to bed with a headache. It is something between them. That is all I can say. You are kind, Angie, to let me share these private matters with you, and you must trust that you can do the same with me."

Of course I could not tell her what I had learned from Momma, and it made my heart sore to keep a secret from this girl who had so willingly told me one of hers. "Eleanor," I said instead, "will you come and help me, even if it means we may be caught and punished?"

She looked alarmed. "What crime would you have us commit?"

"Oh, not a crime, nothing dangerous, more a minor transgression. I just want to know if you'll come and look at something."

She began walking again, but slowly. "What is the punishment," she asked, "should we get caught?"

I shrugged. "It won't kill us."

"Oh!" she said, her hand flying to her mouth. "Your father! So it is true what you said, that the newspapers are wrong and he has not been murdered?"

"That is what I want you to help me find out, Eleanor. Will you?"

She walked along silently for some time. "My mother desires to send me east to finishing school," she said at last. "And to pay for it from her own inheritance. Oh, I long to do it. I dream of it every day. But my father says he cannot bear to lose me, that I have no need of more schooling, and of course his word is law. Nevertheless there is great . . . discord . . . over this in our house. So far my mother has held firm despite the torments of their arguments. If I were involved in a scandal or wrongdoing with you . . . Angie, my mother is not well."

I understood. The rats of worry nipped at Eleanor in the dark night, as they did at me with Papa gone. She would be taking the risk of adding to her mother's burden if she were to help. "Your poor mother. I'm almighty sorry to hear this, Eleanor. But there will be no wrongdoing on our part," I said, "although in truth I cannot promise there won't be a scandal if we are caught. But would not your mother be proud of you for helping me seek justice?"

She smiled in a musing, troubled way, then nodded, and put her arm through mine. "Angeline, you are a forward, cheeky girl, and because of that — though he would never reveal it to you — my father would not like you. Let us go."

I had never thought of myself as forward or cheeky, or that being so would gain me both a foe (Eleanor's father) and a friend (Eleanor herself). But most surprising was the way the words also described Ling Loi and thus, strangely, how she and I must be somewhat alike. Though if cheekiness were a commodity one paid for, I believe that it would be considerable more costly for Ling Loi than it is for me.

Eleanor and I returned to the alley behind the undertaker's shop. As before, it was easy to sneak in through the back door. Today the caskets were arranged differently, and we had to search among them before we found the one marked with my father's initials. But this time the casket had more heft, and I began to dread the next step: opening it to look inside.

Yet Eleanor was eager to leave this room filled with the dead and their spirits, the gloom and the embalmer's sickening chemical smells. She lifted the lid without delay and we both peered in.

The dead man had a reddish-gray mustache, a curly beard on his cheeks, and a shaved chin, just like my father, but he was a good deal older. His nose and forehead were both small and bulgy, unlike Papa's high forehead and long nose.

"This is not Patrick Reddy," Ellie whispered, frowning. Papa was a familiar figure in Bodie, and anyone would have recognized him.

I clasped my handkerchief, filled with relief. "No, it is not."

She straightened up, looking outraged. "We shall tell Mr. Ward of this mistake immediately," she said.

"No!" I said. "For plainly he already—"

At that moment the door in front slammed and we froze when we heard a man saying something about ". . . that cowardly 601 business." If a bear could sing, that is how it would sound—a deep, soft, musical rumble with claws and teeth and power behind it. It was Antoine Duval's voice.

Another man answered, "It's no concern of Wells Fargo and Company, Duval."

Ellie turned to me, eyes wide, finger to lips. She leaned close to my ear and whispered, "That's my father!"

I nodded and said, "The other one is a Wells Fargo clerk. Antoine Duval." The men continued arguing.

"This is a rough town, Tucker, with a lot of wealth coming out of the ground every day. The bank has vested interests."

Mr. Tucker laughed. "The bank doesn't have to worry about the 601 Vigilance Committee. I told you that already. Sometimes a town *needs* its own citizens to be vigilant."

I couldn't read Ellie's expression. She stood motionless, listening.

Antoine said, "In the middle of the night? Wearing masks? I'd wager the town doesn't really want a handful of its citizens to deny Walheim or anyone else a fair trial."

"And I'm telling you — warning you — that the bank's interest is banking. *Not* starting a panic over scrip."

"You have it backward, Tucker. Production

in the Standard Mine is slowing down. It's no secret the mine is running out of gold. But the company — guided by you, one of its major shareholders — is continuing to pay the miners with scrip."

We could hear the fury in Mr. Tucker's voice when he answered. "You know that's how it works, Duval, in all the mining districts during a boom. There isn't enough U.S. currency flowing in for us to cover our payroll. But once the bullion goes out on the stage, the currency comes in."

"Except," Antoine said, "at some point the banks will no longer trust that you can back that paper with gold. Your scrip will lose value and we will have no choice but to refuse to exchange it for U.S. currency. If that starts a panic, and it could, it won't be the bank's fault."

I thought I understood, now, why Ling Loi and I had seen that notice at the Occidental Hotel, and why Mr. Johl wanted regular money from his customers. The mine owners were betting that more gold would be found, enabling it to pay its workers, but businesses were calling their bluff.

The door slammed again and I figured from the hard clanging ring of his boots on the wooden floor that Sheriff Pioche Kelley had come in. I heard that he hammered nails into the heels so you'd know when he was coming. Something like a glass or a gun was slammed onto a table. Then the sheriff spoke. "So accordin' to the doc, Pat Reddy's body was delivered to you for embalming, Ward. Is that correct?" He talked almighty loud, like he worried folks wouldn't listen otherwise.

Mr. Ward answered, "The doc . . . of course, Sheriff." Whether he was selling a cradle or a coffin, he spoke in a mournful, gloomy manner.

"It's been in all the Bodie newspapers," the sheriff bawled. "And on the front pages in San Francisco and Sacramento as well. The whole town'll be at the funeral and then a long woeful wake in the saloons." The sheriff tapped a boot heel on the floor, like a teacher using a wooden ruler to get her scholars' attention. "And every man who ever even thought of stepping on the other side of the law will raise his glass in sorrow.

Some will want to avenge his murder. Tell you right now—I'll be takin' off my badge that night, and God help us all."

The reason the sheriff said that about how sad and mad everyone will be is because of Papa's reputation of never having lost a legal case in California and the territories. I guess Sheriff Kelley decided God would have to be in charge of keeping the peace during Papa's wake.

Mr. Ward made little murmuring noises. He had a way of sending your own words back to you by repeating them. "Glasses raised in sorrow, oh, yes. Every glass. A fine man, Pat Reddy, a fine, fine man. A close friend. Would not have liked that raid, nor sending the Walheims packing." After a pause, he said, "As to the funeral services you ordered, Mr. Tucker—"

"I want a brass band and the finest horses hitched to your fancy hearse, Ward," Mr. Tucker said. "I will pay all expenses."

"Why would you do that, Tucker?" Antoine asked quietly.

I knew why: because he had caused my father

to lose his arm in that hunting accident. But we did not get to hear his answer, as Eleanor put her mouth to my ear and whispered, "The curtain twitched. They may be coming back here!"

Eleanor pulled me out the back door and then we walked around to Main Street, on which the shop fronted. I guess we both wanted to see what would happen when the men came out. "Aren't you going to tell them it's not your father in that casket?" she asked me.

"No, because I don't know whether it will help him or hurt him," I said, hoping that was the right decision. "Act calm," I whispered. "We're just taking a walk."

The sheriff and Antoine emerged from Ward's Furniture and Undertaking onto the wood plank porch. Several idle-looking men were already there, occupying chairs Mr. Ward had out on display, drinking from pocket flasks. Seemed like a lot of people were still arriving in Bodie and finding neither gold nor work. Eleanor and I continued to stroll toward them. Tempers flared easily and brawls were not unusual on Main Street, and we knew girls and women best not get in the way. But I had to try to find out why Papa was going to have a funeral when he wasn't dead.

As we approached, I saw Antoine Duval looking our way. He bowed. "Miss Angeline," he called. The other men stared at us. "I believe your father's funeral is being planned. Please give your mother my condolences once again."

He was rewarded with a shove by a deputy with hair like straw and a big, ruinous nose, who said, "Don't be mocking the bereaved, you mud-caked piece of jerky, or I'll arrest you."

I nodded at Antoine Duval but did not acknowledge the deputy. My father has said that some men who enforce the law are little better than those who break it, and this deputy had tossed a match onto the kindling of my temper. As has happened before, my indignation overcame my public shyness. "Mr. Duval," I said, "are you in trouble? Are you in need of a lawyer?"

"Not yet, miss," he said. All the men laughed. I flushed, for it was as if they shared a joke I was too young to understand. Mama would have seared them with her eyes and her beauty and then turned away to remove herself from their vulgar presence. That is what she would have expected me to do, too.

But Papa says the voice can be a powerful weapon, if aimed right. Eleanor moved closer to me. I saw from the corner of my eye that her chin was high so I copied this position.

I said, "Because Patrick Reddy, Esquire, would be glad, I'm sure, to represent you, should you ever require his services." More laughter and some exchanges among the men that we could not hear and clearly were not meant to.

"Ain't that just like a daughter of Pat Reddy," Sheriff Kelley remarked, "talkin' her head off on some subject on which she is dismally ill-informed. Sorry to say, your daddy's dead, miss." He didn't sound too sorry. Ellie squeezed my arm, which reminded me not to answer him.

Mr. Ward emerged from inside the shop, and with him a well-to-do man I had seen before. "That's my father," Ellie said. Like her, Mr. Tucker was tall with elegant posture, well-kept and well-dressed. He had the bearing of a powerful man accustomed to being in command. I was not at all sure I wanted to meet him.

Then a strange thing happened. Mr. Tucker abruptly let out a loud, high moan and clutched his chest. Ellie broke from me and ran to him as he cried, "Hope is piercing my heart!" This odd, strangled lament, uttered with the anguish of someone bereaved, brought sudden tears to my eyes. His knees buckled just as Mr. Ward pushed a rocking chair under him from behind. Ellie kneeled beside him. "Oh, Father! Father! Get a doctor, please, someone," she said, placing her hand on his chest.

Mr. Tucker leaned his head next to hers and rested his cheek against her hair. He did not look ill so much as surprised and afraid, as if he'd been ambushed.

After a moment he took something from his pocket and shook it in his hand as if he were going to roll a pair of dice. He'd regained his normal voice when he said, "Eleanor, my dearest girl, you know I don't want you walking on Main Street. It's dangerous. Stay home with your mother."

"But then I wouldn't have been here when you needed me. I will get some of these men to carry you to the doctor."

He said, "No, Eleanor, nothing a doc can do. Go home now, go home. Do as I say."

"Come home *with* me, Father. Let me help you," she begged, pressing her face into his chest. He raised her chin, frowning. "I said, go home. I have more business here." He opened his hand and there on his palm was a pair of dice that shone as if they were made of pure gold. He stood, his expression once again stern and distant. But I saw in his face a sad weariness.

Ellie seemed to gather herself. She pressed her handkerchief to her eyes. "Oh, Father," she said with feeling. "I cannot bear to see you suffer as you just did. Are you truly recovered?"

He shook his dice. "It was a momentary pain. Go now."

She rose, gave him a last imploring look, and returned to me, the front of her skirts soiled from kneeling on the dusty porch.

We walked away from them in silence. When we came to my street I began to say my good-byes, for I needed to check on Momma. But Ellie surprised me by asking if she might accompany me home.

"But he ordered you to go home, Eleanor. You had better obey him," I said.

"I know I had, but, Angie, a stronger force compels me to go with you."

"'A stronger force'?" I frowned at her, amazed that she would disobey her father's command. "It seems unwise . . . ," I began. She looked so stricken that I added, "But of course you are welcome. Yes, come home with me."

As we walked, she told me that her father was often with those men, who were not real depu-ties. Some of them were miners who were angry because they had lost their jobs.

"But his attack?" I asked. "Has that happened before?"

"Yes, at home, never in public like this. There is something wrong but he won't speak of it and

he won't allow my mother or me to speak of it."
Her face, usually so serene, was for a moment a
map of worry. She kicked aside a broken bottle in
our path. "But what about your father? And why
would there be another man in the coffin that's
supposed to be his?"

I told her Papa must have some kind of plan
about letting people think he was dead even
though he wasn't, maybe so that lawbreakers will
be less fearful, less careful . . . maybe letting things
get worse so they could get better.

She shook her head. "I don't really understand
these fathers of ours," she said, and I agreed with
all my heart.

Now I must stop, dear diary, for this one long
day has already taken me many days to record,
and what follows will require the greatest of
fortitude to write. I must leave myself time for the
whole story.

Later

I wanted to show Eleanor the envelope I'd seen in Papa's antechamber, sealed with wax and marked "601" on the front. Once I made sure that Momma was comfortable, I asked Ellie if she would come with me to the little locked room. Though she had never been there or heard it mentioned, her head turned exactly in its direction and she stared fixedly toward it, like a dog will do when it hears a sound, inaudible to humans, on the other side of a wall. She nodded gravely, as if gathering courage. All this would have seemed strange to me had I not myself already sensed some kind of presence and otherworldliness in Papa's study.

It must have been the particular slant of sunshine through a window that made the words on the plaque glow, as if hammered out of gold. They, the words, invited Truth to enter and be witnessed. Eleanor seemed blinded by them momentarily, as she stopped and looked down at her feet, blinking, then back at me. "Angie?" she said, and her voice sounded so odd. She searched my face, as if to be sure of who I was. "Water?" she asked in that same tremulous voice.

I looked down at a little stream of clear water emerging from beneath the door. It flowed, contrary to God and nature, around our shoes, not touching them.

I had smelled that water before; now I saw it, and the sight made my throat clamp shut; I almost couldn't breathe. Yet Papa had led me here; I knew he would not let harm come to me. I felt cloaked in his protection. "Nothing in there will hurt us, Ellie," I said, trying to sound calm. "It is only the truth."

She grabbed my wrist as I reached to put the key in the lock. "But there is *water* coming under the *door*!" She danced back a bit, lifting her skirts, and the water still flowed around her shoes, not touching them. "And"—her voice was like a sob—"it does not cause us to be *wet*!"

"I'm certain it is just some kind of illusion, Ellie," I said, as if speaking of a drama where clever manipulation behind the curtain fools the audience. "Or . . . a vision." In fact, my heart thumped around in my chest like it was trying to escape. "But it is for you to decide. You said a stronger force than your father compelled you to come here. Do you want to go home now? Or do you want to find out what is in the room?"

She stood gazing at me, still clutching my wrist, caught between some invisible force that pulled her in and her own natural reluctance to face whatever awaited us. In truth, I hoped she would be sensible, for I felt I might bolt at any second. I was rooted only by trust in Papa and loyalty to my friend. One word from her would have sent me gratefully to the safety of the kitchen.

She nodded, as if coming to a decision, and touched the inside of my wrist to her cheek. A wave of hair had come loose; she pinned it back and said, "Let us be bold, Angie. It is not by chance that we are here. In we go."

But when I unlocked the door and we stepped inside, she took in her breath and stopped in her tracks. "Oh, Angeline," she said, "Oh, dear God."

"What? What is it, Eleanor?" I surveyed my

father's disorderly stacks of papers and folders. Nothing worthy of alarm — unless you counted the stream running through the room, and I had already determined to ignore it.

"Do you not see it? The little pool upstream? The —" She covered her eyes.

I feared she had gone mad and then there it was, past my father's desk and off in the distance: a large puddle, a place where water from the stream collected on the side and was still.

"A tiny child," Eleanor whispered.

Gradually I saw it, too, as if emerging from a mist. A girl barely old enough to walk, toddling along beside the stream, her back to us. She headed toward the puddle, beautiful tiny red leather shoes on her feet, a hooded red cape tied under her chin. I would have gone to pick her up but held back because I knew, despite what I saw and heard with my own full senses, that this was a place and a time I could not and should not enter.

Eleanor began crying softly, sobbing against my shoulder, as the child fell into the water. Helpless to help her, we watched as she struggled and then floated facedown. She sank, weighted by the wet woolen cape — a bright red smudge at the bottom of the shallow little pool. We heard a wailing, keening sound from far off.

Then the child rose up, water streaming off her, and turned and looked directly at us for the first time. She reached for us, and her eyes were not eyes at all; they were black holes in her face. Eleanor screamed, and I felt the small hairs on my arms rise.

Then, as abruptly as it appeared, the scene vanished. No stream, no pool, no red-cloaked little girl with black holes for eyes.

Eleanor and I rushed for the door. It had closed behind us, and at first I could not get it to open. Panic rose in me as if I were being pursued by death itself; both of us scrabbled at the knob. I feared that Eleanor would wrench it out altogether but then finally we were quit of the room, slamming the door behind us, me inserting the key with unsteady hands and then dropping it in my pocket as if it were hot as a burning coal. In the kitchen, as she struggled to stop a ceaseless flow of tears, I gave Eleanor a clean handkerchief, a chair, and a teacup; my own hands trembled as I boiled water for tea. Finally I said, "Do you know her, Eleanor? Do you know the child?"

She shook her head, but then her eyes lost focus, as if they were looking in instead of out. "I . . . seem to, or perhaps I once did. It is as if I *should* know her, yet never in my life have I seen her before today."

I tried to reassure her, and thus myself, that it was only a trick of the mind: There was no stream, no puddle, and no tiny child in Papa's antechamber.

She looked back at me with pity and disbelief pooling as tears in her eyes. "But a trick of *both* our minds," she said. "We were called here, as witnesses, to a place where Truth may enter freely. You know, don't you, Angie, what that poor child is seeking?"

I did, because it shines like gold on Papa's plaque. "Justice," I said. I could not get that ghost baby's terrible eyes out of my dreadful thoughts. "I would do most anything to help that child."

"Of course you would, Angie," she said. "But now, I think, it is up to me."

Soon, overcome by exhaustion, she left for home.

How can I continue to live in this house, walking past that door, after seeing what I did? Why have I not revealed this strange and dreadful occurrence to Momma? Dear diary, a story is unfolding, and Ellie and I were somehow meant to be drawn into it. But Momma, I fear, would collapse from the terror of it, added to her weak constitution, the infection, and worries about Papa. Then, too, it was me to whom Papa entrusted the key; he must not want to worry her. Thus one more secret must be held in my heart.

Monday, June 14, 1880
Dear Diary,

Papa's funeral took place without any of us in attendance, himself included. Today Momma's good friend, the widow Sally O'Toole, came for supper, and how glad I was to bask in her cheerful good gossip and kindness. She seemed to spread warmth and light in the house, chasing all traces of the frightening ghost child apparition away.

She began by asking how she might help us during this strange time of Papa's supposed demise. For Momma had entrusted her with the truth: that we remain certain Papa is alive. "Do tell us about the funeral," Momma urged, "so that we can later recount the story to Patrick."

To amuse us, Mrs. O'Toole provided a lively account of his wake, which all her boarding-house lodgers attended. She said that from what she heard, Papa would have enjoyed the festivities. Mr. Ward drove his elegant hearse with its curved, etched-glass sides, pulled by a team of four gleaming black horses and followed by a long line of mourners. The casket with that other poor unfortunate man in it, the one who really was dead, got buried in the cemetery up on the hill, a place with a beautiful view that the occupants, unfortunately, cannot appreciate. Then it seems a great deal of whiskey was consumed, florid toasts were proposed, and guns were fired at ceilings all night long in every saloon in town. Grown men openly cried at the loss of Bodie's greatest criminal lawyer.

I thought to myself, *But what is Papa's plan? How might I help him?*

I had made cabbage salad and mutton chops and lima beans, which I served with Momma's pickled onions and brown bread. Mrs. O'Toole had also brought a sweet roasted piñon nut cake nestled in a Kuzedika basket — she had traded with an Indian family for both the piñon nuts and the basket.

Momma is still taking in very little food, so I ate her share of the cake.

Sally O'Toole is a cheerful and tireless person who always finds time to help others, even though her eight boarders require constant looking after. (This day she set out a cold buffet and told them to serve themselves. She said, sighing, that she hopes her crockery survives the evening.)

It's well known that each of her boarders has proposed marriage to Mrs. O'Toole, some of them several times, and one, Mr. Gibson — a coachman and stage driver skilled with horses, mules, and donkeys — proposes regularly every fortnight. Plump, pretty, and young, Mrs. O'Toole always says eight boarders are easier than one husband, and more lucrative, too. She has a firm way with the men that keeps them in their place.

I'd been hoping Momma and Mrs. O'Toole would exchange beauty secrets, as I know only those listed in Momma's book, *Practical Housekeeping, A Careful Compilation of Tried and Approved Recipes*. How often I have examined the chapter titled "The Arts of the Toilet," yet the cure for freckles (grated horseradish in buttermilk) did not work in my case. Nor did the recipe for hair oil (two teaspoons each of castor oil, ammonia, and glycerin, enough alcohol to cut the oil, and two ounces of rainwater), which made no improvement other than pasting down my wispy bangs most unflatteringly.

But instead of revealing beauty secrets, Mrs. O'Toole admitted that she could no longer abide those most favored subjects: gold and the stock market. "'Tis all the boarders speak of," she said, ticking off topics on her fingers. "Grubstaking, prospecting, discovery, claim-filing, claim-jumping, mining, refining, assaying. Talk of gold is passed around the table as often as the saltcellar, and it seasons everything they say. Who lost it gambling, who got robbed of it, which woman was made a widow because of it. And every day, after the news from the San Francisco Stock Exchange arrives, oh, my. Did the market rise? Did it fall? Will it recover? Now they're all worried about the Standard Mine. Last week it was the Mono." She turned the plain gold wedding band on her finger. "I hope, sweet Angeline," she said, "that you will not tie up your future to some man's pursuit of gold."

I looked at my lap, mindful that Mrs. O'Toole's husband and dozens of others had been killed in a hoisting accident a few years ago, when an ore cart fell 1,000 feet down a mine shaft. "It is dreadful that your husband lost his life because of gold," I said softly.

"Yes, to be sure," she said, "my Tommy was killed in '78, just like W. S. Bodie himself perished back in 1860 — died, the two of them, pursuing the shiny stuff."

"'Looking for color,' they call it," Momma said.

Everyone knows the story of how our town came to be. W. S. Bodie (some say he spelled it "Bodey" or "Body") was just another prospector, like so many others. He found a deposit in the middle of nowhere, filed a claim, was about to get as rich as Midas, and then he and his partner met their first winter here. Bodie expired in a snowstorm. The gold-seekers that rushed here named the camp after him.

"I heard that those who discover rich deposits always die tragically," I said.

Mrs. O'Toole clucked her tongue and arranged the ruffles of her blouse like a hen preening its feathers. "Oh, it's superstition, no doubt, but don't forget what happened to his partner, E. S. Taylor."

"Killed in his cabin a couple of years later. They say people passed his skull around like a souvenir for years, and it was as smooth as a billiard ball." After a moment I asked if Mrs. O'Toole's boarders were superstitious.

"Oh, yes, especially the miners. No women may ever enter a mine for fear of bringing bad luck, for instance. They take more stock in luck and chance than in common sense. Gamblers they are, even if they never touch a pack of cards or a pair of dice."

I listened carefully to Mrs. O'Toole's stories as I wanted to put some of what she said in my Horrible skit about the Authentic Life of a Western Mining Town. It is, so far (nearly two pages of handwriting), both deeply tragic and richly comic. I am calling it *The Bold Bad Boys of Bodie*.

I asked her what she knows about Sheriff Pioche Kelley's investigations of Papa's murder. She told us that according to her boarders the sheriff has been very busy, having arrested one man who was serving on a jury in Bridgeport that week, another who was in the hospital with a broken leg, and another who had actually been in jail. As soon as each suspect was subsequently released, the sheriff got to work finding his next one.

"My joke teller, Mr. Silus Smith — a carpenter with more fine wood shavings on him than dust on a burro, but otherwise a fine clean man in his habits—he said, 'Everyone knows no one in his right mind would murder Pat Reddy because Pat's the only lawyer could get him acquitted for it. Maybe the sheriff should go arrest someone in the San Francisco asylum for the insane.'"

Even Momma laughed at that, but then she turned serious and shocked me by admitting how weary she has become of Bodie shenanigans. Did she mean Papa? But then she said if it *wasn't* for Papa and some of his friends, the town would be ruled by backbiting and corruption and thugs.

"Well," said Sally O'Toole, "sure in some ways it already is, and thank God the Reddys are on the side of justice." She meant both Papa and Uncle Ned, who is in Leadville, Colorado, looking for silver.

I am almighty proud of having such a famous father and uncle, and I have saved every newspaper story written about them — of which there are plenty. Papa is the more hand-some of the two brothers, but Uncle Ned the more jolly; neither of them is afraid of a fight, though both prefer a fair game of cards to settle an argument. I believe the only thing either of them ever fear is hurting Momma or making her mad.

I got Momma and Mrs. O'Toole talking about the Fourth of July masquerade ball, and Momma said she intended to go, whether or not Papa had decided to return to the land of the living.

"Oh, my dear, you will have tongues wagging," Mrs. O'Toole said. "But if your husband is behind this supposed murder of his own self, would he not want you and Angeline to make believe he is truly gone?"

I started at that, for Papa had never asked us to lie or pretend. Momma seemed equally taken aback. "Oh, no," she said. "Patrick would never expect us to fake widowhood and mourning. I'm certain he's trying to confuse his enemies." She looked bemused. "Anyway, it's well known that we pay no attention to gossip and innuendo—people already consider us a bit scandalous. For Angie and me to attend the ball may be shocking, but it won't surprise anyone."

My hands tingled a bit as if in memory of the

paddling by Miss Williams. Oh, how I hope that Papa *will* be back in the land of the living for our country's birthday!

"And if you wish to be mysterious," Mrs. O'Toole said, "just wear a mask." She told us she is making her own—a hen with an elaborate feathered headdress (which I believe suits her perfectly). Momma and I have not decided what masks we'll wear with our best dresses. Mrs. O'Toole smiled at me and said a masked ball gives a shy girl a chance to be someone she ordinarily is not, someone daring and adventuresome!

Then Mrs. O'Toole kissed our cheeks and cheerfully offered to help us wash the dishes. But we would not allow that, of course. Before Mrs. O'Toole left she presented the intricate and finely woven Indian basket as a gift, which gave Momma the greatest pleasure.

After we tidied up and put everything away, I decided to ask the question that haunted me. "Momma," I began, "did you know that the door of Papa's antechamber was locked the day of his supposed murder?"

She did not. So Papa must have locked it himself before he got murdered, and then he had the key brought to me. I told Momma about Ling Loi's delivery of his "message," and that I subsequently went into the room. I did not mention the envelope I discovered that first night, or that I returned with Eleanor Tucker. I longed to tell her of the terrible vision we saw, but I knew she'd be overcome with horror and worry. Instead I said, "Ellie Tucker visited here Friday while you slept. I like her."

Momma looked at me closely. "So you have become friends with her. I hope you remembered not to tell her anything of the past. It would do her no good to learn from you that her father has been keeping what happened a secret."

"Not a word of it, Momma," I said. "Eleanor and I saw him at Ward's and he had a strange, painful kind of attack—but then he was all right and didn't want a doctor. But—" I broke off, wondering if I ought to tell her.

She knows me too well. "'But'? What is it, Angie?"

"Well, I took Ellie with me to look inside Papa's casket again. This time there was a stranger in it. Now Ellie knows Papa's not dead, too."

Momma shrugged. "No one seems to care that his own wife and daughter don't believe in that cooked-up murder. I guess it doesn't matter."

I was relieved that she wasn't angry. "But, Momma, it's all madness. Do you think it would help Papa if we tell the sheriff all that we know?"

"No. First, because the sheriff is a fool, as Mrs. O'Toole made clear, and second, because your father does not wish us to, and we must trust that he has his reasons," Momma said. "You are not to interfere, Angie, no matter how mad it seems to you."

"But, Momma—" I was going to explain that Papa surely needed my help, or he would not have sent the key to me, but for once I stopped my tongue in time. Papa must not want to worry her; he must want me to act in complete secrecy. This I resolve to do.

Thursday, June 17, 1880

Dear Diary,

Momma has been caught in an uncharacteristic lethargy these past days, as I believe Papa's absence weighs on her as much as the lingering infection. Each day I have accomplished my usual tasks and most of hers as well, with the result that I haven't had the courage, dear diary, to be faithful to you in many days. Yesterday, wash day, I rose at 4 A.M. to start the fire, haul water from the well, and set it to boiling in the great tub. I washed sheets and linens and clothing until time for school, leaving the great, wet, wrung-out bundles to be hung when I returned. Still the day was exceedingly warm and windy, so once I got the laundry on the lines, all was dry by sundown. This morning I ironed for several hours but more awaits tomorrow, as I had to quit to bake bread. I count upon Momma's full recovery soon, not only for her sake, but, ungenerously, for my own.

Now, however, I confront yet a more difficult task, for the Committee of Arrangements for the Fourth of July Ball and Parade is holding its second meeting this evening and, long ago, Momma had pledged her help. Since she is still not herself, she asked that I go in her stead and I could not refuse her.

I wore my school calico and decided to curl the short fringe of hair over my forehead. But I allowed the tongs to get too hot once again, and thus ended up with singed, burnt-smelling bangs. I borrowed Momma's hat to conceal this and set off for Sally O'Toole's boardinghouse, where the meeting was taking place. Eleanor was also attending with her mother.

All the ladies offered condolences for Momma's difficulties, and expressed dreadful sorrow for the loss of my father. I thanked them, for it is impossible to continue to explain that a person is not dead when all the rest of the world attended his funeral and believes he is.

From leftover wallpaper folded accordion style and discarded slats of wood, Eleanor had made two beautiful fans; she presented one of them to me as a gift. I believe they transformed us from schoolgirls into women as we gave languid glances to each other from behind them. This planted an idea about masks we needed for the masquerade ball; I resolved to ask Eleanor about it later.

Mrs. O'Toole got the meeting started right away, the sooner to return to her labors of cooking and cleaning for her boarders. She began by reminding us of the committees: There was the Invitation Committee, the Reception Committee, the Entertainment and Band Committee, the Floor Directors Committee, and the Most Beautiful Costume Committee. Each committee required a volunteer to supervise it and many hands to make the work lighter.

Eleanor gave me a devilish look and whispered, "There should be a Grace Hoop Committee!" A small corner of my mouth smiled at her, because I'd been thinking the same thing: the secret thrill of the game of grace hoop. I'm determined this year to be bold enough to participate, and to join the circle and catch one of the barrel hoops with my two sticks — as long as the boys play fair and do not all throw their hoops at the same time. The reward if you succeed — by sending the hoop back to its sender — is a kiss. I wondered if Antoine Duval would play the game and then I wondered why I wondered that! Behind her fan Eleanor whispered, "Dare you to volunteer!" and I rolled my eyes at her. She knew I would never have the courage to speak at this meeting unless spoken to, much less mention a game for which the prize is a kiss.

So then Eleanor and I conferred seriously and agreed to work on the Invitation Committee. Momma had asked me to volunteer her for the Reception Committee.

As this was being discussed and we all signed our names to duty rosters, Mr. Eli Johl quietly slipped inside, his huge butcher's hands making the cap he clutched look like it belonged to a boy. He had very little hair on his head but a great deal on his face — big muttonchops, a thick mustache, and huge bushy eyebrows.

I guess most everyone knew him and surely everyone liked him, as Momma and I did. Yet several ladies opened their fans and murmured together behind them. "What is everyone whispering about?" I asked Eleanor.

Eleanor glanced at her mother across the room, serving tea and little cakes, and then she leaned her mouth next to my ear. "His wife, Mrs. Lottie Johl, used to work in one of the brothels on Bonanza Street," she said very quietly.

I looked at Eleanor and my wide eyes asked to know more. She leaned in and whispered, "Mr. Johl met her there and fell madly in love with her. It's not that she is so especially beautiful, but she's graceful like a dancer. And she paints landscapes — when you see one you cannot tell she is not a famous artist. *And* she can work as hard as a man and wins at any card game. They got married several years ago, and Mrs. Johl became a proper wife, working in the butcher shop with Mr. Johl. But my mother says some of the ladies claim she can never be respectable because of her past life."

I was thinking about this when Mr. Johl cleared his throat.

"I come to make a contribution." He peered

down at his stained and bloody apron, as if realizing suddenly that he'd forgotten to remove it after closing his shop. "For the parade and the ball," he continued. Mrs. O'Toole clapped her hands once, excitedly. Mr. Johl gave a slight smile, bowed his head, and went on. "A fine, large pig. I will roast it for the town picnic."

Mrs. O'Toole said, "Oh, Mr. Johl! Sure this is most generous. Will we be asking a very small sum for each plate of food and donate the proceeds to the school? Miss Williams has been pleading for books and a blackboard. Grateful she'll be, as we all are."

In a discreet way for me alone to see, Eleanor turned one of her hands palm up and blew on it, recalling Miss Williams's enthusiastic use of the paddle. Ellie can behave in the most shocking ways, thus her friendship is delicious like forbidden candy. I stifled a groaning kind of laugh by turning it into a cough. Then Eleanor and I shushed each other, for Mr. Johl was not finished. He produced a worn bill from within the brim of his cap.

"And . . . this. One hundred dollars in United

States currency to hire the Vaudeville Combination from San Francisco," he said. "Bring them here and let them try to outdo our Horribles."

We all laughed, recalling town celebrations when the audacious Horribles lampooned the mine superintendents and other prosperous people of the town, including Eli Johl himself. Now that I had found their advertisement on the ground, I nursed a powerful ambition — but not, as Momma and Papa hoped, to become a nurse! It was to apply for the position of playwright, as soon as I finished my *Bold Bad Boys*. Of course, no one knew who the Horribles were, and one benefit of working among them would be to discover their identities.

As everyone clapped, Eleanor and I turned to each other in wonder. One hundred dollars was a great sum. The Vaudeville Combination advertised in all the newspapers, a famous troupe that provided much merriment with banjo playing, drama, farces, and dances. Our Bodie Fourth of July was going to be more spectacular than ever before.

Mrs. O'Toole said, "Blessings on you, Mr. Johl. It's a grand donation, isn't it, that tops all the other contributions combined. Sure you're an inspiration and a fine example."

Mr. Johl said, "Ha!" and laughed in a good-natured way and continued, "So: an inspiration? An example?" Then he swept his eyes over the room. I glanced around as well, and saw that many had picked up their knitting or mending, and avoided returning his gaze. He cleared his throat again and rubbed a meaty hand over his bald pate. "There is one favor. Invite my wife, Lottie, to join this committee. She wants . . . very much . . . to help. She is a hard worker and will do anything needed."

Our hostess flushed deeply. "Well, of course —"

"Yes, of course —" Mrs. Ward, the undertaker's wife, began at the same time.

"— of *course* Mrs. Johl *would* be welcome, but there are simply no more slots to fill," Mrs. Rawbone, the dentist's wife, interrupted. "Please do not make this difficult, Mr. Johl. You can see for yourself on these rosters that every possible opening has been signed up for by our experienced volunteers." He took the papers she held out but only glanced at them before thrusting them back at her. He wiped his hands on his apron as if they'd been soiled.

Mrs. Fahey, an assayer's widow, and Mrs. McPhee, wife of one of the biggest shareholders in the Standard Mine, folded their fans with the sound of two smart slaps. Mrs. Fahey declared, "Kindly allow us to respect our high standards of decorum, modesty, and morality while celebrating our country's birthday." And Mrs. McPhee added, "Exactly my sentiments. This is a respectable family event. Perhaps some other occasion would be more appropriate for Mrs. Johl's participation. After all, there are *some* things you cannot buy."

The room filled with the hum of ladies murmuring to each other. I thought several of them looked embarrassed, some sad, others indignant.

Mr. Johl cleared his throat. He coughed and then he got a handkerchief out of his pocket and stood there by the door, blowing his nose. He seemed to go on blowing it for a long time, and none of the ladies looked at him except for a flicker here and there. Something was happening in the room that I didn't quite understand, but it unsettled me. Without thinking about it, which Momma says is one of my gravest faults, I stood and began to move around the outside of the circle, making my way unobtrusively to Mr. Johl. I came up quietly beside him and patted him on his arm, for he seemed like a great big, very sad, very mad, little boy.

Softly I said, "You have inspired *me*, Mr. Johl." The parlor had suddenly gone silent. I knew all were listening to me and the blood rushed to my face. Mr. Johl folded his handkerchief, and I noticed a bit of fancy embroidery: his initials. Did Mrs. Johl have any female friends at all to share her company while doing needlework? I thought how lonesome it would be to do such tasks by oneself. It was Mrs. Johl's fine, lonely stitches that pricked at my awkwardness and made me continue.

"Surely the Invitation Committee would be pleased to have Mrs. Johl's guidance and expertise as an artist," I said. Mr. Johl stared at me in some amazement. Faltering only a little, I finished, "Please tell her that I will call upon her as soon as my mother is better." I pulled Momma's hat low over my forehead and tried to conceal myself behind a standing coat rack, as I felt all the eyes in the room fastened intently upon me.

He pulled aside his apron, returned the handkerchief to his pocket, twirled his cap, rocked back on his heels, waiting—it seemed to me—for someone else to say something. No one did. I felt as if I could scarcely breathe. "Miss Angeline Reddy," he finally said. "My Lottie . . . my dear Lottie will be glad and thankful to receive you."

Then Mr. Johl surveyed the room one more time, nodding as if to himself. "So. Now I understand your meaning when you speak of high standards. My fat little pig will be just right for the occasion. Roasted"—he looked straight at Mrs. Rawbone—"with respectability. Basted," he said to Mrs. Fahey, "with morality. And served"—he caught Mrs. McPhee's eye—"with modesty. Ladies, I hope you will each enjoy a large portion. Good evening." He dropped the money on a small table, jammed his cap upon his head, and left us, closing the door with a thump.

Now all eyes in the room were looking elsewhere than at me. Eleanor had gone to her mother, and the two of them seemed to be discussing something; then Eleanor looked up, clasping one hand tightly in the other. She smiled at me and I guessed she wanted to stand beside me. I smiled back at her and nodded slightly to show that I understood.

But the other ladies reminded me of one day with Papa in the Mercantile General Store at the time he was defending Sam Chung, accused of murder. The customers had turned their backs, murmuring. They shunned Papa as if he had broken some important rule. It made me faint and sick; I wanted to leave the store but Papa had laced my arm through his with no move to go. "Angie," he had said, "'Once more unto the breach,'" which I remembered came from Mr. William Shakespeare's play *Henry the Fifth*. With those words, King Henry rallied his soldiers to gather their courage.

I wished King Henry or Papa or Mr. Shakespeare were there with me at the Committee for Arrangements meeting because "once more unto the breach" is almighty hard all by oneself. I folded my arms, which would have shocked Momma by its show of defiance — but in truth I was close to humiliating tears. "I shall leave now, too," I said.

"Wait, Angie," Sally O'Toole called, beginning to make her way to me. But the other women's disapproval was like fire, flaming my cheeks and pushing me away.

As I reached for the doorknob Mrs. Rawbone's voice stopped me. "Angeline," she said, "please visit with Mrs. Johl if you must, but do remember that the Ball and Parade Committees are formed and organized only at our meetings here. You are not to engage Lottie Johl in our work. Undoubtedly she means well, but we do not need her help."

Gaiety and loud laughter from the saloon next door contrasted with the mood of the committee women. I hurried across Main Street, dodging a team of four mules that pulled a wagonload of vegetables.

When I reached the sidewalk I found myself suddenly surrounded by a group of men, boxed in by them as if by accident. Not alarmed, for even at night Main Street is thronged with people, I began to stride faster so as to break away from this group. However, as much as I tried to dart to one side, or slow down, or speed up, I was corralled like a colt by some very skillful cowboys.

And they surely smelled like cowboys! Their odor was as strong as if they'd smeared themselves with horse manure. Their dark hair and whiskers were (to put it politely) untrimmed, and with their black, wide-brimmed Stetson hats pulled low it was difficult to see any faces. In fact, they all looked the same, in stained blue denim pants, brown vests, homespun shirts, and hairy faces. And strangest of all, they herded me along without saying a single word, eight or nine men keeping in front, behind, and to the sides of me, walking in close formation and facing straight ahead — they could have been a marching band.

But this was no band, there was no music, no talking, and no one looked directly at me.

Just as I was about to try to make a break for the nearest door, I felt a smaller hand grasping mine. Ling Loi, appearing out of nowhere! I gripped her hand tightly, for I had begun to feel a kind of panic and was much relieved to see her.

"Stop bolting," she said, as if being abducted in plain sight by shaggy madmen was merely a lark. "Just walk with us."

"Ling Loi, I will not yield to this kidnapping, or whatever it is." I stopped and they all stopped, too, but one of them moved to my other side and slipped an arm through mine. I tried to jerk it back, but he hung on.

"My dear Miss Angeline," he said in a deep gruff voice I did not at first recognize, "you are the special guest of the Horribles, and we will try our best to give you a Horrible experience. Just one request, please — no kicking. My shin is still sore from the first time."

I stared at him. The mocking smile . . . Though I could not see the scar running through his eyebrow, there could be no question who it was: Antoine Duval.

A tall man at the back said, "It will be Horrible, but is she ready?"

Someone to the side said, "Well, she ain't Ned Reddy!"

Someone else said, "And she sure ain't Pat Reddy, neither!"

"Ridiculous," Antoine said. "She is *Miss* Reddy, you fools. Otherwise: our Miss Take."

Ling Loi snorted.

"Let us go wherever we are going," I said. "All I fear is more such Horrible puns." We all began walking again, but I was no longer uneasy. Ling Loi and I were invisible, walled off on every side by our companions. We reached King Street, the Chinese quarter, and I wished we could have stayed there. The smell of foreign herbs and spices and cooking made my stomach clench with hunger. I heard the strains of a Chinese guitar mingled with the creaking of signboards that hung in front of shops. Bodie is full-to-bursting with people from all around the world, but here in Chinatown nearly every person I glimpsed beyond our escort was Chinese. It was like entering another country.

"Ling Loi," I said, "will we see your parents? Is this where you live?"

"My parents are up there." She gestured to our left, raising her arm toward the hill outside of town.

"The cemetery?"

She nodded and seemed to shiver.

I did not know what to say to this, being ashamed that I had not, until then, thought to ask. It would have been exceedingly rude to inquire as to when and how her parents had died, though I wanted to know. Finally I asked, "Who takes care of you?"

"I'm under the protection of Sam Chung. Do not ask further questions, Angie."

As I'd seen before, Ling Loi became agitated and almost angry when the conversation concerned her personally. I squeezed her hand. "Everyone in the world comes here trying to make their fortune—I mean not just to Bodie, but also to the other mining camps. Must be almighty sad to be far from home and missing your own people."

She narrowed her eyes at me as we walked. "It's harder for the Chinese."

"Well, why don't they learn English and dress like everyone else? Why do they live all together on King Street instead of in town like us? See, if I lived in China—"

"What? You would turn yourself into a Chinese?" Her tone was disbelieving, and she was right—I would want to remain myself, not try to be like them. "Listen to me, Angie. We live on King Street because we are not wanted in town. Everyone here is trying to make enough money to pay back their credit ticket, or to pay for their relative's ticket—the money they borrowed for the voyage to come here—or to send back to family in China who are starving. Chinese are not allowed to work in the mines. We wear our own clothes because we do not want to be like you. And no one wants to die here."

"But *you* were born here in Bodie, so is it not different? Truly, home, for you, must be not China—where you have never been—but California?"

"I told you—no more questions."

Somehow, I wanted her to claim Bodie as her real home. It seemed important to me that Ling Loi feel she belonged here. "But you are not starving. You have work, and friends, and . . . your protector. Surely you must call Bodie your home."

"I call Chinatown and Bonanza Street my home," she said.

I shivered, remembering Miss Williams asking if Ling Loi were living "in squalor." "Well, at least your poor parents are at peace," I said.

She wrenched her hand out of mine. "At peace! At peace! Buried here? All they wanted was to return home to Kwangtung. My father came like everyone else, to make his fortune. He never planned to stay. He and my mother would have wanted to be buried with their ancestors. Do not tell me they are at peace, for they are not!"

Stunned by this outburst, I was silent. A driver hauling wood passed us. Men carried vegetables and dried fish in buckets suspended from long wooden poles they balanced on their shoulders. I tried to imagine what it was like to be Ling Loi. It seemed she had nothing, no one, no rich nugget of home to keep safe in her heart. Yet I'm certain it was not pity she wanted.

Soon our troop turned onto Bonanza Street, which is also called Maiden Lane — the part of Bodie forbidden to me. The streets were lined with pleasure palaces and I thrilled to this new adventure. Yes, I could claim I was herded there against my will, but that is not the entire truth. In the midst of a street famous for sinfulness, I craned my head, hoping (in vain) to see something scandalous as we walked. "Where are we going?" I asked, shouting to be heard over the blaring sounds up and down the street: music spilling out of the saloons and dance halls, raucous drunken conversations, horses pulling carts and small coaches, and of course the booming from the mill.

"Yes, where shall we take this arresting young lady?" the tallest one asked.

"*I* am arresting? Clearly it is you who have arrested me," I retorted.

"Then we shall take you to jail, of course," said Mr. Duval, and ever so slightly tightened his grip on my arm.

The jail loomed at the farthest point on Bonanza Street, after all the pleasure palaces, the end of the line for many whose pursuit of amusement verged into lawlessness. Our little band swung around to the back of the jail, and Antoine Duval let out a low whistle.

A man emerged from the shadows. He was dressed just like the others, and like them had a full beard—though his was reddish. He smiled at me. My escort melted away and I ran to Papa.

Later

I confess that the days of anxious concern, the work of the house that stole hours of sleep, caring for Momma, the terrible ghost child, worries about Ling Loi, poor Mr. Johl—well, all of it turned into tears and poured out of me. Papa held me tightly in his one arm and waited as I cried and cried. Suddenly aware of all the Horribles standing apart at a short distance, I mopped my face with a handkerchief, blew my nose as discreetly as possible, gulped air, and forced myself to calmness.

"My darlin' brave Angel," Papa said, calling me by my pet name. "It's almost over. Tell me quickly: How is your mother? Has her gum healed?"

"You know about that?"

"Well, surely you don't think I would leave the two of you in a wee boat with no oars. I've been close by. You were as brave as a man the other evening, standin' your ground out there on the porch with the old revolver." He tugged my earlobe gently. "And as foolish."

"Papa! You were there!"

"Yes, with Antoine."

"Can you not come home to us? We have no money and the apothecary is loath to extend more credit for her medicine, which she craves at times. Please, Papa, please come home."

"Soon," he said. "Meanwhile I must remain dead and you must remain resolute. But Ling Loi should have warned you about the laudanum!

Did she not explain that your mother would become dependent on it?"

I thought back to that day after Dr. Rawbone lanced Momma's gum, when Ling Loi first appeared. Looking around, I saw that she was gone again. "I did not pay any mind to her warning, Papa, though Momma realized lately that she wanted it too badly and is not taking much. But what does a girl like Ling Loi know about medicine?"

"A great deal more than you, my dear Angie. The ingredient in laudanum that kills pain is opium. You know about the opium dens in Chinatown. Ling Loi has seen many people addicted to opium, and most of them die. What about Emma's wound, my dear young nurse?"

This made me cry anew, though not for the reason he must have thought. "Oh, Papa, truly I have no gift for nursing, though not through fear or squeamishness." I could think of no way to tell him I'd rather play word games with the Horribles than become useful and practical like a nurse. I sighed and said, "I think her gum is improved yet her spirits are low. But how do you know Ling Loi? Did you know that her parents are dead and that she may be sent away?"

He took the handkerchief and gently blotted my wet cheeks. "A remarkable child. I knew her father, Lee Wing, who accumulated heavy debts before he was killed in an accident hauling wood. He left a widow who died a few months later when their child, your friend Ling Loi, was born. That girl has had a most . . . unusual history. You should ask her about it."

"She'll hardly tell me anything! She appears and then she suddenly disappears when you don't expect it. I think she's afraid and brave at the same time."

"With good reason." Papa touched my singed bangs and said, "You must go. Tell your mother I will be with her soon. There is money—the scrip that was supposedly stolen when I was murdered. It should still be good at the shops and markets, same as regular currency." He told me where it was hidden in his antechamber.

"Papa," I said hesitantly, leaning into him,

"have you ever noticed anything . . . strange in your antechamber?"

I felt him tighten, like someone preparing to receive a punch in the stomach. "Yes, I have, darlin'. A presence I can't see. A small presence. And something else, something lunatic, and you would understand it no more than I do."

"I understand more than you know. You ask me to trust you, and I do with all my heart. Please trust me, too. Tell me, Papa."

He pulled on his beard and nodded. "Water," he said. "A stream. A puddle. At first I only smelled it and then there it was, running through the antechamber."

"And though it touched your shoes, they did not get wet. I have seen it, too."

"I don't know whether to be relieved that I'm not insane or worried that we both are," he said. "We will speak no more of it." I would have told him about the ghost child if he'd asked, but he did not. He seemed to want to shake it off, like a dog wet with real water. "Now tell me this: Did you find the sealed envelope?"

I told him I had, and had guessed the significance of it. Papa looked around. No one was close by, but he leaned in and spoke right into my ear in a low voice. "Angel, never let that envelope leave my room; keep it safe until—" He whispered that I should bring it with me on a certain date that I dare not record in case anyone should find this diary.

He hugged me again fiercely. "Now you have spent a little time with the Horribles. How was it?"

"Horrible," I said, smiling. I realized that the cowboy clothes and horse manure was a kind of costume, the beards or wigs and hats a kind of mask. "But I like them! They seem to make a joke of everything!"

"In fact, not everything. They've kept an eye on you and your mother—oh yes, I know about both times you snuck into Ward's back room."

"Papa, you have been spying on me!"

"Darlin', I need to know that you are safe, even while I myself am forced to stay hidden."

I looked around for Antoine Duval and saw him leaning against a corner of the jail. "Is that why Mr. Duval was outside Dr. Rawbone's office with that giant man?"

Papa nodded. "Yes, with Big Bill Monahan. Antoine is a detective, though he calls himself a clerk. Wells Fargo put him at the head of a special investigation of stage robberies, and his job at the bank gives him opportunities for running many sorts of errands in the streets of Bodie."

This news made me feel discouraged and disappointed. While it appeared that my encounters with Antoine Duval occurred by chance, I'd secretly hoped that he arranged them because he was fond of me. Now I knew that he was only keeping watch over me for Papa, as if I were a child.

Papa pulled a cigar from his pocket and rolled it between his fingers. One of the Horribles strode forward as if to light it, but Papa waved him away. "Be careful, Angie. Because it is believed that I am dead, with Sheriff Pioche Kelley easily bribed, a few desperate men are probably going to try to take over the town. They believe, according to our spies, that no one will stand up to them. If you need to get a message to me, tell Ling

Loi or Antoine, no one else. Do you understand?"

I promised solemnly and threw my arms around his neck. "Papa, please try to finish being dead soon. Can we not just leave all this trouble and move to San Francisco? Surely you would find all the clients you need there, without the worry and lawlessness of Bodie. Please, Papa."

"Right you are, sweet Angel," he said, and sighed, and kissed me. "But, darlin', it's your courage I'm counting on to see this through. Just to stir the pot a wee bit and see if justice rises to the top. Are you with me?"

I dreaded putting my courage to the test, as it is something I sorely lack. And whatever little I did have was used up earlier at Mrs. O'Toole's. Yet I could not deny Papa, who was living a furtive life in hiding. "I am," I said to him, and added in what I hoped was a brave Shakespearean voice, "'Once more unto the breach.'" He smiled at that.

Ling Loi returned, carrying a large and lumpy flour sack. "Those scoundrels in jail got you to take their laundry, I see," Papa said. "What're they paying you?"

She flashed a rare smile. "Plenty," she said.

Papa nodded, looking pleased. He kissed my wrist and the entourage returned, surrounding Ling Loi and me once again.

We left her on King Street. As I was escorted the rest of the way home by the horrible-smelling Horribles, a light breeze lifted some of the manure scent.

It also lifted a curtain in my mind, the curtain hiding a secret.

I knew this was one secret I had to reveal.

When Antoine Duval fell into step beside me, I spoke to him as if we were already in the middle of a conversation. I intended this as a witty and sophisticated mannerism that I hoped would show him I was not merely a child to be guarded. I said, "It's called *The Bold Bad Boys of Bodie*."

"What is?"

"A Horrible new skit."

"Ah."

"It's about the Authentic Life of a Western Mining Town," I explained.

"I see. It's presumably written by someone with experience, insight, and firsthand knowledge."

This made me bristle, as he seemed to be mocking me. But I reminded myself that making fun is what the Horribles are about. "Yes, all that, plus punishing puns and devilish deeds."

"So it's about boys playing at vigilantes? Is that what the play's title signifies?"

I blushed and did not reply, for I had indeed described an actor that holds his pants up with one hand and his gun with the other.

"Miss Angeline," he said, "we like to skewer the rich and mighty. It would not be suitable to poke fun at boys caught playing at dangerous games. That was a mistake they regret — or at least I know for certain Hank does."

I saw he was right and resolved to take that part out, though it would mean recopying everything once again. "What about a deputy who walks around with his palm out, demanding bribes from everyone he meets?" I had not

148

realized the others might be listening to our conversation until one of them laughed.

Antoine grinned. "That's the idea," he said. "What else? Is there a story to it? Audiences like stories."

"The playwright is not sure about the actual story yet," I admitted.

"Tell me this," he said. "Three things about life in Bodie."

The breeze blew fine dust like a curse in our faces. I could feel grit collecting, as usual, behind the collar and under the cuffs of my calico. My other everyday dress needed mending, which I would have to do tonight in order to wash this one. "First," I said, "work and dirt."

"Dirt!" echoed one of my escorts. "Oh, yes, Bodie is dirt, mud, muck, grime, and filth. But it's, pardon me, more a concern of women than men."

"And it is not something funny," Antoine added.

"I think I can make it so," I said, more confidently than I felt. "The deputy is dirty. Dirty clothes, dirty job, dirty conscience."

A giant man in front whom I knew to be Big Bill Monahan, Momma's guardian angel, stopped and turned around. He said, "You got that tin badge with you, Butte?"

The man called Butte pulled something out of a saddle bag and handed it to Mr. Monahan, who pinned it to Antoine's shirt. It was an enormous sheriff's badge, the size of a dinner plate. "You got the role, Duval."

Antoine set his hat on the back of his head, the way the sheriff wears his, so his whole face was visible. My eyes were drawn to the thin white scar running through his eyebrow.

"I otta arrest you, you mud-caked piece of jerky," he said, extending his hand to me, palm up.

"Hold on," I said. "Turn sideways to the audience with your back to me and stick your hand out behind you." He did. "Clink, clink, clink," I said. "Coins falling into your palm."

"He's taking bribes and doin' somethin' else at the same time," someone suggested.

"Yes," I said. "With your other hand, unlock the door to a jail cell. Clank, clank, clank."

The men laughed.

"Out comes a big, tall, clean, rich man," I continued. "He throws paper money, scrip, all over the stage. It's worthless." Remembering what Mrs. O'Toole's boarder had said, I added, "The deputy shoves a poor old sick man who can hardly walk into the cell. He's coughing." Two Horribles immediately acted these roles, adding their own words and exaggerated gestures.

I was filled with a new and thrilling sense. We were sketching out a play, and they were waiting for *me* to tell them what should happen.

Antoine said, "So, Bodie is work and dirt. What else?"

"Gold. Everything that happens in this town started with gold," I said. "Everyone who's here came because of the gold, even people who don't work at the mines, the ones who sell vegetables or practice law or ride around in the middle of the night wearing masks." I thought a minute. "We start with . . . a bank clerk. He's bald and fat and bad-tempered."

Antoine said, "Hey! Wait a minute!"

The men laughed again.

"It's true-to-life," someone said. "Tell us the rest."

"Am I hired?"

Antoine frowned. "We never had a *female* write the skits before," he said doubtfully.

"She's only a schoolgirl," the man called Butte added.

"But," Big Bill Monahan answered, "there are always a lot of women in the audience. I think they'll like a skit with dirt and work and gold in it. I bet Miss Angie has seen and heard a few things while scrubbing the floor and shaking out the rugs. And she can make up a nom de plume so no one'll know our playwright isn't a man."

Antoine shrugged and looked uncertain. "Need to think about it," he said. "Meanwhile, let's get the 'playwright' home." We resumed walking but in looser formation. Antoine Duval and I didn't talk until he said, "You haven't told the third thing."

Smarting from his dour response to my Horrible ideas, I said, "A heart injured by fierce indignation."

"Ah," he said. "That's good." I didn't know whether he meant it was good I'd used some words from Swift or that he agreed with the sentiment.

We had arrived at my home. When I left the Horribles, some of them bowed to me from the waist and doffed their hats with mocking but good-natured exaggeration, actors acknowledging a schoolgirl playwright.

One of them even blew a kiss. I have no idea which one it was.

Saturday, June 19, 1880

Dear Diary,

Eleanor begged me to visit her, for strange things were happening at her home. She would not reveal what sort of things, but her distressed and mysterious air drew me. As soon as I arrived, Mrs. Tucker clasped me to her and said how proud of me she had been at Mrs. O'Toole's boardinghouse. Then she collapsed in a chair and tears started in her eyes.

"Oh, Mother, please don't cry now," said Eleanor.

"You are right, dear, it is unbecoming. Yet I must explain to Angeline how ashamed I am of my own frailty. I ought to have allowed Eleanor — and allowed myself as well — to go with you to Mr. Johl. Those ladies are simply cruel. It takes pluck to stand up to them. I most distressingly lacked it." She seemed as if her heart were breaking.

"Oh, Mrs. Tucker," I said, startled and pleased beyond measure to be described as having pluck, "it is so kind of you to say this, but you give me more credit than I deserve. Please do not trouble yourself further. Those ladies at the meeting would scare anyone, I believe — even the Bold Bad Boys from Bodie."

(By saying this, dear diary, I hoped to bring out a smile on Mrs. Tucker's face, for most of us residents tolerate our town's fearsome reputation as reported in all the newspapers. This is said to be the wildest place in the West, plagued by gunfights and lawlessness and treachery of every sort. In fact, all of that is true, as Papa can attest by his many hours in courts of law. But as long as we women and girls do not interfere with those Bad Boys, they are courteous and even gallant in our presence. We are safe enough — or at least so Momma has always claimed — if we stay levelheaded and keep out of the way.)

Mrs. Tucker did brighten for a moment, and then she said she had to hurry to an appointment with Miss Williams to discuss Eleanor's future education. I am trying hard to be unselfish and glad for Eleanor, for it would be a fine thing for her to go to school in the east, yet the idea of losing my new friend pains me.

Almost as soon as Mrs. Tucker had gone we heard a strange kind of moaning from the rear of the house. "What is that sound?" I asked Eleanor, for it was giving me gooseflesh on my arms.

"My father," she said.

"Another attack? Then, Ellie, I must be going." I do not wish to remain in a person's house when her father is moaning. I do not want to know the personal and private reason for this man's misery, especially when he shares a terrible, ancient secret with my own father.

Eleanor grabbed my arm. "Wait, Angie," she urged. "Come see him."

"Ellie! I saw him that other day and it was dreadful. I am sorry for him and for you, but my presence here cannot help." Mr. Tucker, for all his joviality and goodwill, tipping his bowler hat to ladies on the street, was not a person I wished to encounter. A kind of villainous weakness radiated off him like heat. I remembered Momma's warning, that she did not trust him.

"Listen to me, Angie. He won't even know you are there. I need for you to see something. It is a matter of life and death."

It was clear from her eyes that this was the truth; she did need me. Reluctantly, I allowed her to lead me to the back of the house.

Eleanor tapped at a closed door, and there being no response beyond the continual moaning, she opened it to a small parlor. There on the floor, his back to us, sat Mr. Tucker. He sat like a prisoner in a chairless cell, his knees pulled up to his chest with his arms wrapped around them. Hatless, his head seemed smaller, his hair thin, a circle of baldness on top. At first I feared that he was ill, but then I heard the sound of a stream, felt unusual coldness in the air, and caught a glimmer of red.

Eleanor said, "I think it's the little girl." She spoke in a flat tone. Either her father did not hear or did not care.

"Yes," I said, and felt again the profound sadness of the child's torment. "Why — do you not see it?"

"No, at least not so clearly as in your father's room. But I have heard him mumble about the cape and the drowning. My mother does not know about it. He sees the vision only when she is away from the house, and I am certain he hasn't told her." Mr. Tucker reached out his arms, but I knew from his moans that the small child stayed just beyond his grasp. I remembered how it fell into the stream and what would happen next — the silent entreaty, the anguished cries from afar, the terrible black holes for eyes. I could not force

157

myself to stay there, nor could I bear to hear the hoarse sobs of the man on the floor. I escaped, pulling Eleanor with me and closing the door.

"Angie, I cannot abide this," she said, clinging to my hands, once we were back in the front room. "My father is going mad, and although he was always quick to anger and capable of violence, this is now worse. The ghost haunts him continuously. He is greatly frightened."

Eleanor herself was frightened, and no wonder. I asked, "Have you confided any of this to your mother?"

She shook her head. "I cannot. I sense that if my mother learned about the ghost child she would do something . . . dreadful. Perhaps she would turn on my father, and he would . . . it does not bear thinking. I do not know why, but — Angie, you have seen it twice. What can it mean?"

Of course I have wondered this often, dear diary, but it is so odd, so unlike any experience in the past, that I have no answers, and all I see in my mind is the plaque on Papa's door. I stood there gripping Eleanor's hands, trying to think of something comforting to say, when over her shoulder, through the window, a face peered in.

It was Ling Loi.

I ran as quickly as possible to the door and flung it open, but Ling Loi had already gone. There was not a trace of her. I was beginning to feel the most extreme exasperation about that girl. Eleanor wondered aloud why I was dashing about throwing open her front door. Was there another ghost outside? I assured her that this was no ghost, nor anything to fear, and reluctantly said my good-byes, as much work awaited me at home.

Monday, June 21, 1880
Dear Diary,

Moth season is upon us. Last year we had been ill-prepared, nearly losing our only good carpet and our three winter coats, plus Papa's suit for court appearances. Momma and I had spent many hours patching moth holes in blankets and clothing. Now it is once again time to moth-proof the house, and this year I intend to do it well.

I needed to lay down a good layer of ground pepper mixed with camphor gum, strewn thickly under the carpet. This work is strenuous, as the furniture must be moved, the carpet taken up, the floor swept and washed, the anti-moth mixture applied, the carpet laid back, and the furniture restored. Momma is still too weak to help.

I returned home from school along Main Street, which was, as always, clogged by traffic of all kinds. A wide, shallow gulch — which at this time of year is filled with muddy water — runs along the center of the street, and everyone who passes is splashed or even drenched with that foul water. Trying to avoid this (I had no wish to wash my dress and oil my boots), I collided with a passerby and was pushed against Gillson and Barber's general store window. A large man whose clothing had a thick, sweet odor reached down to pick up the school supplies I'd dropped, muttering apologies. While he did this I glanced into the store. I tell you all this, dear diary, so that you will see how it came to be that I spotted Ling Loi through the window, way in the back of the store. Her arm was being clutched in the eagle-talon grip of Miss Minnie Williams.

Mr. Ward, for it was he who had knocked into me, offered to escort me to his business establishment for a glass of water. "Oh, no, thank you, Mr. Ward," I said, trying to keep Miss Williams and Ling Loi in my sight within the general store, which was thronged with customers. "I'm not in the least thirsty."

Mr. Ward put his long, sad face to the window, evidently made curious by my curiosity. Yet I thought it may not be a good idea to call attention to Ling Loi.

"I am most intrigued by that new contraption," I said, and indeed it was true.

"Ah, yes, intrigued," he repeated. "By that contraption. Yes. A shower stall, I believe. Complete with overhead sprinkler."

I shuddered. "How awful! Do you mean that the poor victim stands there while being doused by streams of water?"

"Oh, yes, by streams of water," he said, "poor victim. A form of torture, barbaric, really."

This talk of poor victims directed my gaze back to Ling Loi, held captive by Miss Williams. I knew I had to help her if possible. "Well, good-bye, Mr. Ward," I said. "I know you have to get back to your caskets and . . . things."

"Ah, to be sure. Must get back, now, to a death mask, another gunfight casualty, I'm afraid."

Remembering the lifelike death masks I'd seen in Mr. Ward's back room, I asked impulsively, "Would the same technique be used if you were to make a death mask of a . . . uh, a pig, or, say, a horse?" I did not wish to reveal my true reason for asking.

To my relief he did not at first seem to consider this a peculiar question. "A pig or a horse death mask," he mused. "Interesting. The technique, yes. Quite the same I'm sure, though I have never faced the challenge."

"I am sure you would be equal to it," I said flatteringly. "And that technique, what would it be, exactly?"

"To make a death mask for an animal? Is *that* the technique you wish to know, Miss Reddy?" Now Mr. Ward's soulful eyes widened. He made it sound as if I was going to embark on some bloody pagan ritual — maybe devil worship or cannibalism! He leaned over, putting his face near to mine, as if studying it for my own death mask.

I stepped back, glancing to the side quickly to be sure Ling Loi and Miss Williams were still in view. I decided it would be prudent to tell the truth. "I just . . . was thinking of the masquerade ball." I felt myself blushing to a great extreme, sure he could read my daydreams about dancing with Antoine Duval exactly as if they were printed on my forehead. "My friend Eleanor and I are aspiring to make our masks especially dramatic this year."

He nodded, as if all I'd said made sense. "Dramatic masks, yes, of course I see, Miss Reddy, how death masks would have come to mind, especially having run into me, an expert, if I may say so. Widely recognized as such, I might add.

"But an animal face? Oh, my dear, no. No, I should recommend your *own* face as a mold for your mask. But my techniques, involving plaster and a subject that is, well, deceased, that is, dearly departed, which is to say, and please pardon my bluntness, dead — well, these techniques of mine are not the same as you would use. Muslin strips would be your material, and a paste of flour and water, I should think. Being exceedingly careful not to cover the nostrils." He took in a deep breath, evidently to show me the important function of nostrils and why one should not block them.

"And first, of course" — he touched my cheek with one hesitant fingertip — "a thick coating of liniment, a protective ointment such as a mixture of mutton suet, resin, and beeswax. Or buy a ready mixture called Vaseline at the apothecary's.

"Should you need any . . . *advice*, or any . . . *materials*, or even a . . . *demonstration*, please do not hesitate to come to me." He made this offer in a strange, insistent way, as if he were eager to participate in my pagan ritual himself. Mr. Ward was an exceedingly odd person, in part due to his very awareness of and even pride in these oddities. "Ah!" he cried, straightening up. "Here comes your little friend and your teacher, Miss Williams, isn't it? The pair you have been watching, I presume? Well, I shan't keep you, my dear."

And just as Ling Loi and Teacher emerged from the general store, Mr. Ward lurched off on his stiff, long legs, leaving me gaping after him.

Moth prevention treatment would have to wait. True, I dreaded the work it entailed, but I was fearful that Teacher had formulated some horrendous scheme to send Ling Loi away, so I decided to follow them. What if the girl should suddenly be thrown on the afternoon outbound stage, in the clutches of fearsome orphan-guards (these I imagined to look much like prison guards — bad-tempered and gray-skinned)? If an abduction happened, I would need to hatch a rescue plan on the spot.

Although Miss Williams still clasped Ling Loi's arm, the two walked easily together and carried on an animated, non-stop conversation that I would have dearly loved to hear. Alas, I was forced to remain many paces behind so as not to be discovered spying, as I had been by the observant Mr. Ward. But Ling Loi was swinging her little cloth bag, and I could see her smiling up into Miss Williams's smiling face. All that smiling between them was so strange as to be almost sickening.

At length they arrived at Johl's butcher shop, but instead of entering, they nipped between it and the dressmaker's shop next door, and went around to the back. I turned my head toward the street as I followed past Mr. Johl's window, in case he was looking out. I had done nothing wrong, but nevertheless was seized by a need for secrecy.

I crept cautiously between the buildings, listening for voices ahead, increasingly worried that Ling Loi was falling into Miss Williams's insidious trap. If he were there, my father would have saved her, but since he was not, this task fell to me. I determined to rise above all danger, even though my own life be threatened. Yes, even should I be kidnapped and tortured and mutilated. Thus fortified by my own thoughts, I advanced and peeked around the corner.

Mortification! Waiting for me, hands on bony hips, was Miss Williams herself, whose stern frown smacked me the same as if I'd crashed into a wall. I resisted the urge to flee. Though Ling Loi seemed to have disappeared, I glimpsed a corner of her jacket behind the outhouse.

But then the back door of Mr. Johl's shop opened a crack and the little brown pup shot out in a frenzy of excitement. It found Ling Loi and then took off around the corner at top speed, followed by the girl. Then the door opened fully; the woman holding it was dressed in a beautiful shimmering blue gown such as one would wear to an evening at the theater or, I imagined, to ascend into heaven like an angel. She stepped outside and said, "Oh, Miss Williams! How kind of you to have brought a friend."

Miss Williams said, "You mean Angeline? But I—" She stopped in apparent confusion.

The woman was looking at me closely. She smelled partly like the puppy and partly like grasses that grow at the edge of a stream. The corners of her mouth curled up and her eyes crinkled at the edges, as if she had a private, funny secret. Despite that amused look, her nose was straight and severe, her eyebrows wistful, her honey-colored hair a flounce of curls that shone in the sun. They were the type of curls, real ones, that never needed the heated clamp of a curling iron.

I tried to smooth my frizzled wisps of bangs, feeling nervous and shy. She grinned suddenly and said, "Angeline Reddy! You're the one who had the courage to speak publicly on my behalf at that dreadful Committee of Arrangements meeting. Oh, Eli was so grateful! He said either he would have roasted those women on a spit or they would have skinned him alive." She clasped my two hands in hers.

So this was Mrs. Lottie Johl! For some reason, even though we were right at her door, I was foolishly, unreasonably, unprepared to see her. Had I expected her to remain hidden in her husband's house, afraid to show her face to proper society? Had I thought she would be poorly mannered, dressed in undergarments, smelling of whiskey? Such is the attitude of those respectable ladies, and in some way it must have spilled into my own suppositions. Relieved at her warmth and humor, I squeezed her hands. And then she glanced over my shoulder—and fainted.

Ling Loi, who had evidently returned, dashed around behind Mrs. Johl, helping me to keep her from falling to the ground. We sat her down, and the dog licked her ear while Miss Williams patted the unconscious woman's hands and cheeks, none too gently I might add.

But most surprisingly of all, Ling Loi burst into tears, burying her head in Mrs. Johl's neck and crying as if she had lost—or found—the only thing she ever loved.

Miss Williams put a stop to that by issuing orders: I was to fetch a glass of water and Ling Loi was to cease crying at once and use her handkerchief properly. No command was given to the dog, who was apparently beyond reproach. At that point, Mrs. Johl regained consciousness and sat up. She stared wide-eyed into Ling Loi's face and then she gathered her in her arms, the two of them rocking and hugging each other in a way so sweet and passionate that I almost could not look.

And now I am so weary, dear diary, that I must resume this account tomorrow. I will close with the good report that I completed the moth treatment, and in addition have added bundles of dried sage, thyme, and spearmint to our clothing closet, and Momma said I accomplished it all in a most efficient and practical way.

Tuesday, June 22, 1880
Dear Diary,

Now to continue the story of Ling Loi and Lottie Johl (known as Lottle), as it was revealed to me.

We sat on straight-backed chairs in the Johls' parlor, which was crowded with a very great amount of furniture, lamps on every table, crocheted doilies under every lamp, vases, figurines, and glass bowls filled with hard candies. For being so full, the room felt uninhabited, like a stage setting after the play is over. On the walls hung paintings in great gilded frames, etched-glass mirrors, and a curious portrait of a full-bearded man.

Ling Loi sat on the carpet facing Mrs. Johl. The two of them spoke animatedly for some time, Mrs. Johl having asked about some women she called "the other mothers."

"Oh, Lottle, it is mostly so sad. Ellen Fair was beaten and murdered by that wretched man, Jon Draper, who is in jail in Bridgeport awaiting his trial. Sunny Mollie was clubbed over the head and robbed — they don't know who did it — and later she took too much opium and died. The doctor said she had a disordered brain." Ling Loi had begun to cry again, and Mrs. Johl rocked her for a bit, an expression of great sadness on her face.

"I read in the newspaper about Julia being arrested," Mrs. Johl said quietly. "Arrested for vagrancy!" she explained to Miss Williams and me. "Oh, the dreadful unjustness and shame of it all! Abandoned by husbands, all three, Ellen and

Mollie and Julia, and them only trying to survive."

Ling Loi pressed a handkerchief against her eyes—I know the gesture myself, as if it could somehow keep the tears from leaking out. "Nell McCloud was caught stealing firewood and had to choose between a forty-dollar fine or forty days in jail. And she being so frail with her bad foot! She was freezing in that little cabin. She had no money, so was sent to jail. I went to see them both, Nell and Julia. They shared a cell so at least they had some company."

Mrs. Johl sat with her back straight, her head bowed. "Poor Nell. Such a hard life she's had." Cupping Ling Loi's chin in her hand, Mrs. Johl said softly, "And Popo? Is she all right?"

Ling Loi nodded. "Strict, like always. I am learning the Three Obediences and the Four Virtues but she says I have to work harder on 'pleasing manner' and 'reticence.'"

Mrs. Johl smiled and so did I. Miss Williams's eyebrows twitched. Popo surely had an almighty challenge in trying to teach those things to Ling Loi.

"And who is this person that has taken on such a formidable task?" Miss Williams asked.

"Everyone calls her Popo. It means grandmother but she's not my real grandmother. She was a friend of my mother's."

"And she became my friend, too, when we got to know each other," Mrs. Johl said. "She's a dressmaker. One day I went to her for a fitting, and there was a tiny infant with her. She allowed me to hold the baby. Through gestures Popo made me understand that the child's mother and father had died. After that, Ling Loi and I spent much time together."

In a small voice, Ling Loi said, "Until Mr. Johl came and took you."

"Please try to understand, Ling Loi. I am so fortunate—Mr. Johl has been good to me."

"That's what the other mothers explained after you left," Ling Loi said. "They said he made a condition to being married—that you must walk away and never go back to Bonanza Street or to Popo's, and never visit any of us, not even to say good-bye. You had to put that life behind you. I did not understand! It felt like if you had died. Because . . . because . . ." Ling Loi seemed to be struggling for words. She went on in a burst, ". . . because having so many mothers is harder than . . . anything! Already three of them have died, even though I didn't know the one I was born out of, and the one I loved best, besides Popo, left me." After a pause, Ling Loi said, "And I know it is not obedient and shows lack of a pleasing manner, but I hated Mr. Johl for taking you away."

Mrs. Johl hugged Ling Loi again, and I, very carefully, without moving my head toward her, looked over at Miss Williams out of the corner of my eye. She was holding the puppy and caressing it, and, like me, listening.

"Mr. Johl wants only my happiness. But for me, too, it has been hard. More than you know, Ling Loi." She cleared her throat. "We will talk more in a little while. Now we must not keep our visitors any longer." She looked at Teacher. "All right, Miss Williams. Please explain your mission and I will do what I can to help."

"I am most concerned," Miss Williams began, getting right to the point, "for the child has come under the notice of the Presbyterian Mission Home in San Francisco. Perhaps that is where she should go, though I would have thought it better for her to remain with her own people. Yet it seems she has no family here."

Mrs. Johl looked angry. "She has no *relatives* in Bodie. But Popo and Sam Chung and her mothers at the Palace are her family."

"How is it," inquired Miss Williams, balancing her teacup on one knee, "that Ling Loi speaks and, according to herself, reads English?" Miss Williams did not excuse herself from asking direct and personal questions, as I have been taught to do. I believe this is a bad result that comes of being a teacher. But I was glad she asked, being myself interested in the reply.

Mrs. Johl sighed deeply, playing with Ling Loi's long braid. "My visits to Popo were an excuse to be with Ling Loi. Popo saw how much I loved the child. She trusted me."

Miss Williams waited.

Ling Loi said, "Lottle, you have to tell all about Sam Chung."

"Sam Chung. Yes." Mrs. Johl's mouth tightened for a second, as if the words were reluctant to come out of it.

"One day when Ling Loi was about a year old I paid a visit and found Popo to be ill. I returned the next day to see if she needed anything. Sam Chung was there. He spoke English and I knew him slightly from his store, the Emporium, so I told him how fond I'd become of Ling Loi, and asked him questions about her. He told me that Popo was in charge of Ling Loi's care and upbringing until the age of twelve. Then the girl would work for him because her parents owed him a great deal of money.

"I saw that Popo was worse: ill and feverish. Sam bundled up the baby to take her to another woman until Popo got well. Ling Loi reached for me and I said, 'Let me mind her for a few hours, until you find someone.'

"Sam didn't like that idea at all. He was in a hurry and argued with Popo. I didn't understand

176

the words, but I'm sure Popo was trying to convince him I could be trusted. Later I found out that many people in Chinatown were ill with the same fever Popo had, so maybe he realized it would be hard to find anyone who could care for a baby. Finally he handed her to me.

"I was working at the Palace at the time, and brought her back with me. The other girls loved her instantly, for none of us had ever seen such a beautiful baby, Chinese or any other kind. She was so calm, not a crying type of wee one, and loved being held. A perfect baby." Mrs. Johl stroked Ling Loi's cheek with the back of her hand. It was the most tender of gestures.

"Popo remained ill for several weeks, and Sam Chung himself got the fever. He sent his lawyer, Pat Reddy, to ask me to keep Ling Loi until he or Popo recovered and could come for her. He knew he could trust Mr. Reddy"—Mrs. Johl smiled at me and my heart swelled at hearing Papa's name—"to make sure we understood it was only temporary."

"I cannot imagine," Miss Williams said, "that

the owner of the Palace looked kindly on babies, even temporary ones."

"Oh, you are right about that, Miss Williams. Madame Steele came nigh to exploding, so angry she was. But Mr. Reddy told her we dared not return Ling Loi to Chinatown for fear of catching the illness and bringing it back with us. And then the next day a curious thing happened.

"It was a slow morning in late spring and we were all sitting in the dance hall, Mollie, Ellen, Julia, Nell, and me, doing our mending and watching Ling Loi take her first steps. Even Madame Steele, polishing glasses behind the bar, couldn't take her eyes off that baby. Old Peasley was banging out some Irish jig on the piano. Ling Loi tried to dance and walk both at the same time. She'd fall on her bottom, look greatly surprised, and then pull herself up on the legs of a chair and start over. A couple of prospectors killing time at the faro tables begged to give her a kiss. They'd never seen such a sight as a Chinese baby.

"I made a joke about how much a kiss might

be worth, and one of them brought out a bag of nuggets. He had tears in his eyes, saying he hadn't seen a baby in so many years, and never a 'real China doll baby.' He was an old fool but he gave me an idea.

"During those weeks, Ling Loi earned her keep. Men were willing to pay a silver dollar to kiss her hand and two to kiss her cheek or forehead. They would pay just to smell her baby hair. I believe some of them would have stolen her if we hadn't kept a close and constant watch.

"Naturally we had to give a percentage of this money to Madame Steele. But when Sam finally got well and came to take Ling Loi home to Popo, there was an unexpected bonanza for him. I put the coins and nuggets in a bag, handed it to Ling Loi, and told her, 'Give it to Sam Chung.' She understood perfectly and launched herself over to him all smiling and said, 'Sam Chung!' and dropped the bag at his feet. Those were her first words.

"Well, Sam is nobody's fool. He saw Ling Loi's potential and decided right then that, like him, she should learn to speak, read, and write English as well as Chinese. Of course we offered to teach her. He and Madame Steele made a deal: We would take care of Ling Loi every morning, and strictly supervise her expensive kisses from homesick miners, and begin her English education. She would be returned to Popo each afternoon. Sam repeated that he would allow this until she turned twelve years old. Then he'd put her to work in a dance hall until she had repaid her parents' debt to him. He promised he would not send her to China, nor to a home for orphans in San Francisco."

Miss Williams's hand flew to her heart. "Good heavens!" she cried. "You cannot mean work in a bawdy house!"

As if in a mirror, Mrs. Johl's hand went to her own heart. She wore a ring of faceted clear green stones. "In his mind, he was not being barbaric, only practical. Most Chinese men left wives and families behind. Mr. Chung figured Ling Loi would eventually end up working in a dance hall and he was offering his protection so she would not be mistreated."

Miss Williams had set her teacup on a table. I felt a little sorry for her knee when she pounded it with her fist. "A deplorable situation. Please continue."

"Madame Steele agreed to the deal with the stipulation that she receive a percentage of all earnings for kisses, to which Mr. Chung nodded accord, plus an additional monthly sum for Ling Loi's 'provisions,' which he refused to pay on the grounds that *he* was the one to whom money was owed. Ellen, Mollie, Julia, Nell, and I voted to pay it out of our own earnings. Split among five of us, it was not so much. So Ling Loi had five Palace mothers plus her Popo *and* other mothers in Chinatown during those early years. We all took turns caring for her."

Mrs. Johl sighed and continued. "She was a solemn, serious little girl. She grew up speaking two languages easily, with no effort at all. As she got older we taught her all the book learning we had among us and tried to raise her proper. But we all knew that when she turned twelve she would be lost to us. We loved her but tried not to love her so much our hearts would be broken."

I could see that Ling Loi enjoyed hearing her story told, and that she'd heard it before. She caught my eye when Mrs. Johl described how she got money for being kissed, as she knew I'd only faintly believed her before.

Miss Williams asked softly, "And did you succeed?"

Mrs. Johl make a clicking sound with her tongue. "Five years ago when Mr. Johl and I fell in love, he asked me to marry him. As Ling Loi said, his only stipulation was that I leave my life on Bonanza Street completely, and come to live in his world. In many ways, he saved my life. Of course, neither of us realized how hard it would be for me to make friends among the Christian women here, how . . . lonely it would be. Many times I wanted to go to Ling Loi, for—to answer your question—no, I could not prevent my heart from being broken. But I kept my word to my husband and I shall continue to keep it." She leaned forward and rested her cheek on top of Ling Loi's head. "Some choices can just about pound all the light out of a person's heart, like that ore-crusher up at the mill. Yet we must make the choice to make them."

Miss Williams nodded, her face somber. She stood and went to examine the strange portrait on the wall. With her back to us, she asked, "How has this likeness been achieved? It is finely wrought, yet there is something unusual about it."

"Every line," Mrs. Johl said, "is made from human hair. A cunning artist. But I care not for it. He is merely playing a game with us, with the result that we look at the portrait and fail to see anything but his cleverness. Neither the man in the picture nor the artist himself is revealed."

"You speak as an artist yourself," Miss Williams said.

I glanced at Ling Loi. She had stopped crying, and had composed her face so that no expression could be seen on it. She hid her feelings behind a smooth mask of unconcern.

Impatient, I swallowed a large gulp of tea, wishing they would get back to discussing Ling

Loi's dreadful situation. If she were sent to the Presbyterian Mission Home, she would run away, and probably land in even worse trouble. If she stayed in Bodie, she would soon be put to work in a dance hall. Her fate rattled in my head like dice in the hands of a gambler.

"You have asked me many questions, Miss Williams," Mrs. Johl said. "Now I should like to ask you one."

We all looked at Miss Williams, who lifted her chin slightly, as if she expected something to strike her. Like Ling Loi, I kept my face expressionless, yet I felt glee and triumph in my heart. Clearly Miss Williams preferred to ask questions, not answer them, and it was an almighty rare occasion that I could be there to listen.

"Who is it that contacted the Presbyterian Mission Home, Miss Williams?"

"I am not in a position to discuss—"

"Did you think to help this child, Miss Williams? It was you, was it not?"

Before she could reply, the door adjoining Mr. Johl's shop flew open. The butcher burst into the room and Ling Loi sprang to her feet.

"Ha!" he said, in that way he had of not laughing. "Visitors!" He moved swiftly, for such an ungainly big man, across the cluttered room to the window. Closing the heavy curtains, he said, "My dear Lottie, your guests will have to leave. I have word that the 601 is out on its dirty business again." He eyed Miss Williams and then me. "You are safe, no doubt, but all the same I will accompany you both to your homes."

The vigilantes again. I felt dread as I thought of their masked midnight raids.

Mrs. Johl went to her husband as Ling Loi melted behind a huge overstuffed chair. That girl could disappear in an instant! "Wait, Eli," she said. "Please do not judge Miss Williams by the behavior of her brother. I believe she is trying to do good" — here she glanced at the teacher, who only arched her back further. I was afraid she'd topple backward if she got one bit more bothered — "and the Lord knows it is not easy in Bodie."

"I will be fine, Mr. Johl, but thank you all the

same," I said. "Ling Loi can come with me—"

"Ling Loi will stay here tonight," said Mrs. Johl, looking not at me but at her husband. "Please, Eli. I want her safe with us."

Mr. Johl passed his meaty hand over his large bald pate. Before he said a word, the puppy raised its head and an instant later I heard the back door close. Ling Loi was gone again.

Mr. Johl walked me home in silence and then he and Miss Williams continued toward her house, beginning an animated conversation as I left them. I hoped that whatever Miss Williams was trying to convince him of, she would not succeed.

Friday, June 25, 1880

Dear Diary,

Several days have passed during which I could not write, so now I must record the further events of that afternoon and night.

We ate a light supper of Momma's good Turtle Bean Soup. I know you are wondering, dear diary, so I shall tell you: It is not soup made from a turtle, but regular black bean soup with the addition of a slab of salt pork and sliced hard-boiled eggs, and very good it is for the hungry yet weary.

And such weariness I have never felt, like an ache in the marrow of the bones, an ache in every muscle, even behind the eyes. I fell into my bed and into instant sleep.

She woke me in the gentlest way, so at first I thought it was Momma. Through the bedclothes she took hold of one of my big toes, grasping it lightly as I floated up out of sleep. Although a small candle flickered in her hand, it was dark in the room. She stood by the bed, holding my foot. "Shhh," she said.

"Ling Loi?"

"Yes. Can you get dressed and come with me? Something bad is happening at the Babcockrys. I cannot find Antoine or Mr. Reddy, but I think if you come out, maybe they will find *us*."

The frightened tone in her voice made me come fully awake. Yet somehow it is harder in the night to summon courage; all I wanted was to burrow down deep under the blankets. The thought of pulling on my layers of underclothes and dress and shoes seemed a task beyond my ability.

"I brought you a disguise," she said, and let go of my toe. Over her shoulder hung a bag; from it she took some garments. "Pants and a jacket just like mine, from a woman about your size. Your feet are almighty big so I brought you a man's slippers."

I touched the cotton fabric, which was soft from many washings. It seemed almost more wrong, in my sleep-addled mind, to go out of the house wearing Chinese clothes than to sneak out without waking Momma. (Of course I dared not wake her as she would have forbidden my leaving.) Ling Loi must have misunderstood my hesitation, for she said, "Oh, do not worry. They are very clean — no fleas."

"Ling Loi, be quiet. Bring that candle closer." I began to dress. If she could go running around the streets of Bodie at night, so could I. Dread was strong but excitement and the possibility of dangerous adventure were stronger.

"Hurry," she said. "Please."

The clothes fit me well enough; they were loose, light, and allowed such freedom of movement as a cat enjoys. Even the cloth slippers were large enough for comfort; my feet felt nimble in a way that normal shoes and boots do not allow. It thrilled me strangely to walk in the shoes of a man, as if they gave me a magical power. She tied a black silk scarf over my hair and we made our way silently out the back door.

We blended into shadows and I realized I did not have to walk in the modest, proper way of a young woman. We ran and I leapt as I have not since I was a child. My usual clothing was a suit of armor in comparison. Then a worry came to me, and I said, "Ling Loi, how will my father or Antoine recognize me? And if they do, what will they think?"

"They or their friends have been keeping watch on your house. If they're around here, they saw one Chinese girl go in and two Chinese girls come out."

Our eyes adjusted to the dark, enough that we could dodge around the ruts and mud and garbage on the street. Ling Loi led me through back ways and alleys. I feared no ghosts and no haunts. She made me braver than I was.

A group of rough-looking men approached, hats low and spurs jangling, some of them singing a bawdy song. We flattened ourselves against the back of a building, and they passed by. Their smell of horse manure reassured me, though it was too dark to recognize any of them. One of the men lagged behind the others. "Who goes here?" he asked.

"Wing sisters," Ling Loi responded immediately.

"Taking flight?" He shook his head. "Not tonight."

I guessed what he was from the way he spoke, punning and rhyming. "Why," I said, and hoped he couldn't see my cheeks reddening at the thought of Antoine Duval, "is it a Horrible night?"

"That's right, miss, Horrible," he said. "Back to the nest, you two."

So this was Papa keeping an eye on me with the Horribles' help.

Ling Loi realized this, too. She said, "There is trouble at the Babcockrys'. Can you get a message to Mr. R. or Mr. D.?"

"Trouble?"

"I overheard Constable Kirgan talking about it," Ling Loi said. "Said Mr. Babcockry shot another man over a card game."

"All right. We heard the mob was organizing; didn't know it was about Babcockry. Go back inside." He took us by our shoulders and turned us around, back the way we'd come. "Hurry," he added, and we began to jog.

We turned a corner and Ling Loi looked back. "No one's following," she said.

"Let's go," I answered, and she knew I did not mean home.

We took a circular route to the Babcockrys, who lived in a little shack behind the wigmaker's shop where Bessie Babcockry worked. As we approached we could hear the mob of men in front, out on Main Street, shouting orders and insults. After several thugs with burning torches rushed past, we crept along the alley and ducked into the rear room of Ward's Furniture and Undertaking. This time I had no wish to peer into caskets. I led Ling Loi quickly through the back room and to the front parlor, where we could peek around the heavy velvet curtains and watch the scene on Main.

Men seated on panicky horses fired their guns into the air; others stood in a loose group taking swigs from bottles. They all wore masks or hoods and threw long shadows from the lights spilling out of saloons and dance halls on both sides of the street.

Suddenly, from between two shops, a woman and two boys appeared; they were herded out to the street. It was Mrs. Babcockry, shouting at the top of her lungs. Her younger son — we called him Marbles — in his nightclothes, gripped her hand; each of them carried a satchel. Her beautiful hair shone as if it were lit from inside her, a thick golden cloak covering her shoulders. Marbles looked around wildly, as if seeking some way of escape. Hank Babcockry followed, bound by ropes and struggling uselessly. He had his mother's hair, though his was matted and stuck out in odd clumps. I was glad to see, at least, that his pants stayed put, anchored by Papa's sturdy leather belt.

They were shoved into a small wagon.

"That boy Marbles taught me how to play ringer," Ling Loi said. "We played keepsies and I won a cat's-eye off him. Where are those men taking them in that wagon?"

I didn't know so I shushed her.

"How dare you force us out of our home in the middle of the night?" Mrs. Babcockry shouted. "My *husband* has been a *member* of the 601 Committee! Sure, we got behind on the dues, but he's a right upstanding member of this mining district! Upstanding! Don't touch him, you reprobate!" She directed this to a man who had tried to break her son's grip on her hand. He spat in the dirt. "I'm reporting all of you to the head of this Committee! Oh, yes, I know names! I know who you are! You should be ashamed!" The crowd laughed and shouted at her.

Finally Mr. Babcockry stumbled into view, prodded by several masked men. His clothes were stained and torn, his hands tied behind him, his feet wearing only ragged socks with holes in the toes. He lurched unsteadily and cried out, "Bessie, doncha know yer not supposed to tell people I been a member? That's the very exact reason the 601 wear masks, see? 'Cause they don't want people to know who they are! Somebody give me a drink!"

His wife snapped, "Oh, for the love of God, Bab! It's not another drink you're needing right now!"

One man stepped out from a group of onlookers. He climbed with long legs onto a display of caskets. I saw that it was Mr. Ward, probably keeping an eye on his establishment. "Boys," he shouted mournfully, "I'm always glad for business, but let's settle this the right way. Take the man to the sheriff and leave his family alone."

Mr. Ward astounded me, as even from inside I could tell that the crowd surged with some kind of eager madness. I thought he had better get down from his perch, and quick. But he continued, "Not a good time for business, this sad business especially."

Shouts and warnings pelted Mr. Ward: He was advised, in strong, unrepeatable terms, to mind his *own* business.

"My own business, of course," Mr. Ward repeated, calmly nodding. "But this is the sheriff's business. Where might he be?"

"Seen him over in Molinelli's Saloon, Ward. Get down off yer caskets and go buy him another drink," someone shouted.

"Molinelli's," Mr. Ward repeated. "A fine idea. Let's all go and see what—" Before he could finish, someone lashed out with a mule whip, caught Mr. Ward at the back of his legs, and made him topple off the platform of caskets.

The mob turned back to Mr. Babcockry and, with a sudden rush, knocked him to the ground. Some men began kicking him but I could not see what happened next. He must have been kicked partially under the wagon. Or maybe he scrambled there to try to get away from the attack. Someone threw a bottle that went wide and hit one of the wagon's two horses on its rump. Ling Loi and I saw the horse jerk; we saw the masked driver trying to retrieve the reins that he'd dropped; we saw the horses lunge forward several yards.

Mr. Babcockry lay in the street.

Suddenly the crowd drew back. Someone screamed, "The wheel went right over his neck. Musta broke it!"

Masked men shuffled backward. Began to melt back into the darkness, or duck into the nearest saloon. Those mounted turned their horses away. There was shouting, but it sounded different — less angry, as if the wheel that broke Mr. Babcockry's neck also broke the mob's will. It had been the beginning of something dreadful, and all at once it was the end.

A group of women who had kept themselves in the background came and helped Mrs. Babcockry climb out of the little wagon. I saw Mrs. O'Toole among them; she removed her shawl and placed it over Mr. Babcockry. Someone untied the ropes binding Hank.

I dropped the curtain. Ling Loi took my hand. "That boy Marbles always has a runny nose but he's nice," she said. "Now he doesn't have a pa."

"Nor his brother, Hank," I said. "I'm almighty sorry for them."

As we cautiously opened Ward's back door, I saw a half-dozen cowboys hurrying toward Main. They were panting from hard running. I guess the Horribles, being unpaid actors and punners and poets and protectors of girls, cannot afford to feed and shelter horses of their own. They were too late to help the Babcockrys, even if they could have swayed that mob.

Ling Loi, still holding on to my hand, looked at me closely before we slipped into the alley. "That Mr. Ward was the bravest man we saw tonight," she said.

He was only a strange old undertaker, but I guess she was right. "Braver than Sheriff Kelley over in Molinelli's," I said. "Looks like the 601 run the town now. I wonder who will be next."

We started toward home and my heart seemed to freeze when a few men turned into the alley and approached us, nearly blocking our way. These men were not Horribles, I was sure. Ling Loi said something in Chinese, and I kept my head down as she had instructed earlier. We scrambled to the side and the men, arguing, barreled past us with hard-eyed looks, forcing us to make way for them. They showed none of the gentlemanly manners I'm accustomed to. My Chinese disguise gave me a curious kind of freedom, like being invisible — or as if, in the eyes of those men, I was not worthy of being seen. Now I know that a disguise can hide as much about the wearer as it reveals about the observer.

Ling Loi came inside with me and waited while I undressed so she could collect the borrowed clothes and return them to their owners. Then she left, all on her own, and I watched her jog away into the night. Mr. Ward had been almighty brave that night, but he was not the only one.

Sunday, June 27, 1880

Dear Diary,

It was furious hot in the kitchen. I determined not to think about the dreadful events of a few days ago, to think, instead, of celebration.

Eleanor and I were boiling onion skin dye, simmering vinegar fixative for the muslin, and stewing flour-water paste.

We were making our masks for the grand ball, and we were steaming with pure excitement!

I planned to dance until the moon sank and the sun rose.

But no one would have danced with us if they saw us now! We perspired like horses, our faces were gooey from the protective ointment, and our hair was sticky and powdered with flour.

The cast-iron cookstove heated the kitchen to 100 degrees.

Momma had heard of the arrival in town of a wagonload of fresh fruits and vegetables at reasonable prices. Before she left with her big basket, she presented us with two flour sacks. She had cut holes for heads and arms. To cool off, we removed our outer clothes and wore the sacks as aprons. Oh, the glory and freedom of bare arms and legs!

Once the paste cooled, we cut muslin into strips and dipped them into the mixture. It was sticky and messy and got on everything. I lay on the floor on my back—as far from the stove as I could get—while Eleanor applied overlapping strip after strip to my gummy face.

I stared up at her through my eyeholes. This first layer was a torture of itchiness. I flopped my arms. "Don't be impatient," she said. "Wait for it to dry."

"It's taking almighty long," I said, trying not to move my face while I spoke. After a moment, in as casual a way as possible, I asked, "What if someone I don't care for asks me to dance?" Ellie had much more experience with social events than I had, and she knew the proper etiquette.

"Unless he is drunk or rude, you must accept all offers, and be gay about it. If you decline a man's invitation, do not accept any other man's for that dance."

I fanned myself with a newspaper. "But what if the man you want to dance with doesn't ask you?"

She laughed. "And who would that be?"

Instead of answering, I ran my fingers along the edges of the mask. Dry and almost rigid. "It's dry enough, Ellie, I'm positive. Help me lift it off." Using both hands, she carefully pried it up and placed it on an upside-down bowl.

"The nose!" she cried. "It's all floppy! It's sinking!" She grabbed the saltcellar and positioned it beneath the mask's nose. Once thoroughly dry, we would add a second layer of white muslin strips.

I wiped the ointment off my face while Ellie took my place on the floor. For her mask we used muslin that had been dyed to a bright yellow gold in the onion skin bath. I tried to be as delicate and precise as she had been, molding the strips to the contours of her face.

"Fan me, Angie," she begged.

"'Don't be impatient. Wait for it to dry,'" I teased. As I fanned her, I thought of another question.

"Ellie," I said finally, "what does it mean if a man winks at you? Not at the ball, but just during a conversation."

She smiled, not moving the other muscles of her face. "If we are talking about a certain Wells Fargo clerk, it means he likes you."

"But how can you be sure? He just thinks of me as . . . an Irish satirist schoolgirl."

"Then Mr. Duval must surely love Irish satirist schoolgirls, especially ones wearing fabulous masks. Is it dry yet?"

"No."

"Shall we paste chicken feathers to our masks like Mrs. O'Toole? It could be pretty."

"I want us to be unique, Ellie. Mysterious, shining, radiant."

"Of course! Brilliant, luminous, dazzling! I wish we had jewels we could add."

"Momma would say, 'If wishes were horses, beggars would ride.'"

"My mother, too." We both sighed. "Please can we take the mask off now?"

I pried around the edges with a little butter knife. As I lifted it, I said, "All I want is to dance and dance through the whole night until dawn."

Ellie said, "Oh, Angie, that's it! Our masks will be perfect!"

As we tidied up she told me her idea for our costumes and I felt a thrill go through me. But then I realized what an awful girl I am, with Papa in hiding, and Mr. Babcockry getting killed—and all I can think about is being in the arms of that Wells Fargo clerk with his tragic eyebrow, whirling me around and around and around.

Tuesday, June 29, 1880

Dear Diary,

Yesterday Momma decided to cook larded calf's liver to go with the onions she had bought, and sent me to Mr. Johl's. I was also to buy the bacon to lard it with, and was thinking of how good this would taste as I hurried along Main Street.

The sign in Mr. Johl's window said CLOSED. This was unusual for mid-afternoon; I paused to peer into the window. What I saw shocked me: The meat case was clean and empty except for blocks of melting ice. Mr. Johl's knives and apron were not hanging in their usual spots behind the counter. The shop looked not merely closed — it was deserted.

I ducked around the corner of the building, as before when I had followed Ling Loi and Miss Williams, and made my way through overgrown grasses to the rear. There I saw a wagon loaded with trunks and cases, and Mr. Johl lugging yet another trunk out from the house.

"Oh, M-Mr. Johl," I stammered, flushed with embarrassment at being discovered like a common sneak behind his house. "I . . . I saw the sign in the window and hoped you and Mrs. Johl were not ill, and then I . . . decided to come around to see if . . . there is some way I can help."

"Ha!" he said, as if he had just discovered something. "As you see, we are leaving Bodie."

Mr. Johl had evidently hired a two-horse wagon and a man I recognized as one of Sally O'Toole's boarders, Mr. Gibson, the teamster. He looked up from the hoof of one of the horses and nodded at me. Unlike most men who carry their weapons in their pockets or tucked into waistbands, he wore a holster. Clearly Mr. Johl had hired him as both driver and armed guard. The wagon was piled high.

I said, "I'm almighty sorry, Mr. Johl," and I was. "But what—" I broke off, stopping myself from asking about Ling Loi. I could hardly bear the thought of her losing another mother, one she had just recently found again, one she so clearly loved. But such a question would surely anger Mr. Johl. I said, "What about . . . the dog?"

Mr. Johl stared at me a second, but I could not

read his thoughts. He looked different without his apron. In Levi denims, with a neatly ironed shirt and vest over his substantial paunch, he could have been a prosperous rancher or a banker on his way to a picnic outing. Just then, from within the house, Lottie Johl called, "Eli? The canvases are ready."

He moved toward the door. "My Lottie is fond of the dog. We take our Bonanza with us." Then he added, "It is her little joke, the dog's name."

"Please tell Mrs. Johl I regret that I didn't get to know her better . . . tell her I wish her well," I said. "And . . . and . . . Mrs. Tucker and her daughter, Eleanor, also send their regards, and Mrs. O'Toole, and my mother. I wish—"

"Yes," he said distractedly, and barked the sound that should mean laughter—but didn't. "Ha! We wish, too. But now that they have removed your father, the vigilantes are taking over Bodie. I sell my shop at a loss. Soon scrip will not be honored—it has begun already—and people will panic. It is over. The death of the town of Bodie has begun, and we won't be here to witness its last tortured breath. Good-bye, Angeline Reddy."

Before leaving, I wished Mr. Gibson a safe journey. He was cleaning a shotgun with an oily rag. "It's a dirty business, miss," he said, and wiped his hands on his pants.

Returning home, I wondered how it can be that meanness may be a sin but it is not even a crime. Perhaps it is worse than a crime, for often no justice may be brought—at least in this life on earth.

For I knew the real reason they were leaving. Mrs. Johl would never be fully accepted in society, never have friends among the other women. If they'd stayed in Bodie, their dreams and hopes would have been severed by the keen knife of respectability.

I have pasted below, dear diary, the *Daily Standard* newspaper account of what happened next. Momma always says things turn out as they are meant to, and Papa adds, yes that they will, but only if people do the honorable thing. I can't imagine how that is true now.

HOLDUP ON THE BODIE-TO-BRIDGEPORT ROAD

Odd Discovery in Luggage

Prominent Bodie butcher, Mr. Eli Johl, and his wife, Mrs. Lottie Johl, were held at gunpoint when attempting to move their household from Bodie to Bridgeport.

MASKED MEN

Three masked highwaymen blocked the road and demanded cash and valuables from the couple. Teamster driver Zachariah Gibson of Bodie shot off several rounds that went wild. Rather than returning fire, the highwaymen disarmed him and took his shoes and belt. Mr. and Mrs. Johl were forced to hand over their entire savings.

NO HONOR AMONG THIEVES

Rarely have highwaymen demanded personal belongings of the fairer sex during holdups on our roads. The Johl robbery therefore stands out as an especial affront to women travelers. One of the masked men dismounted and addressed Mrs. Johl, who held a dog on her lap. He is reported to have said, "Give us the ring, the broach, and the hatpin. You can keep the mutt." Mrs. Johl complied while Mr. Johl, who was unarmed, offered several unprintable insults in response. In the course of this, the dog jumped down from the wagon and sank its teeth into the dastard's boot. With the masked men's attention distracted, Mrs. Johl drew a double-barrel derringer from under the seat and shot the hat off of one of the attackers, revealing hair she described as "the foul nest of a rat." She took more careful aim on

the hatless man, who mounted his horse
and fled, apparently unharmed, followed
by his partners.

AN ADDITIONAL SURPRISE

After the highwaymen retreated, a stowaway was found to be hidden among
the luggage and other belongings in
the wagon. He jumped down and ran
in the opposite direction. No description was given but the stowaway is
thought to be a young boy who may or
may not have been in cahoots with the
robbers.

REWARD

Anyone with any information leading to
the arrest and capture of these bandits
should contact Sheriff Pioche Kelley of
Bodie. A reward will be posted.

Wednesday, June 30, 1880

Dear Diary,

When Momma went for a quick visit to Mrs. O'Toole's, I decided to wash the kitchen's wood floor, still sticky and crumbly from the Sunday mask-making project. Some grease stains had to be treated first so I put some lye into the tin cup kept for this purpose and placed it on the stove until boiling hot, poured a little on each spot, and scoured with ashes. Next I filled a bucket with soft hot water and was scrubbing when Momma returned. She brought friendly gossip from Mrs. O'Toole via her boarders; all were talking about the Johl robbery. Mr. Gibson, the teamster, said he had lost both his boots and a friend with Mr. Johl's departure.

I wrung out the mop and began to attack one corner of the floor. Once it had cooled down enough, Momma cleaned the stove. She removed the ashes and cinders from every part, rapping smartly on the sides of the pipes to dislodge the soot that collects there. I watched her curiously, for she beat that stove as if to punish it, as if its heat had transferred to her and raised her temperature.

She got into more of a temper when she discovered that I hadn't saved bits of meat left from supper and I'd forgotten a bar of soap in a basin of water. "A woman can throw out with a spoon faster than a man can throw in with a shovel," she admonished me. "That meat could have made a nice little hash for breakfast, and the soap has dissolved in the water unnecessarily. You must learn to be more thrifty and less wasteful, Angeline." After a moment she added, "I noticed this morning that your dress has a rent in the sleeve and dust on the hem. It looks shabby and poorly cared for."

I felt hurt by this, after all my labors during Momma's illness, but of course I didn't argue. I did not wish to add bad manners to my list of offenses.

Momma swept out the ashes with a long-handled brush-broom and plenty of vengeance. We worked in silence for some time. Then, abruptly, she dropped the broom, sank into a chair, put her head in her hands, and began to cry. I busied myself in the corner, not wishing to intrude — but she continued to cry as if she could not stop.

There can be no more pitiful or frightening sound to me than my mother sobbing uncontrollably. It clenched my heart like a muscle that seizes up. It hurt my chest.

Finally I pulled a chair near to her and put my arms around her, appalled at the meagerness of her shoulders. "Oh, Momma," I said, "please don't cry. What is the matter? Is it Papa?"

My voice must have jolted her out of some deep place of misery, for she gained control of herself and poured water from the pitcher onto her handkerchief. She cooled her face and turned to me.

"Forgive me, Angie. I was wrong to scold you. I am the one who is shabby and poorly cared for. I need your Papa and I curse this town for keeping him from me." She looked at me, her eyes full, still, of tears. "For keeping him from us. You have grown up since he left, and I have gotten old."

I pondered what she said about me, for I felt no different — still a plain-faced, constantly blushing girl with no natural gifts and, in public, a great excess of shyness. I said, "Momma! It's only been a few weeks! We cannot have changed so much in that time!" I jumped up, picturing Papa with a witness, asking the questions that get them to say (or admit) the truth. I propped my foot on the chair, right elbow on knee and pretend-cigar in hand. I rolled the "cigar" between my fingers, smelled it, let my left arm dangle straight down. His stance was easier to imitate than his voice, but I curled my lips in imitation of Papa's winning smile. "Now, darlin', you want me to stand by and watch while the thugs and hoodlums take over Bodie? What kind of husband would I be then?"

"Oh, Angie," said Momma. "You do sound just like him! And you made me remember something one of Sally O'Toole's boarders told her about your friend Ling Loi. She no longer comes to the jail for laundry. She seems to have disappeared.

"On my way home I decided to ask about her, and stopped at several shops in Chinatown, but no one had any information." She paused. "Except at the Emporium. Mr. Chung, the owner, appeared angry at my questions, though he took pains to conceal it. He was very polite, of course—I know he feels grateful to your father for defending him in the three trials. But he seemed to imply that Ling Loi has run away!"

I had told Momma very little of Ling Loi's background and doubtful future. I know she would have forbade me to interfere or become involved, as none of it was my business. Now I was almighty worried about Ling Loi and where she had gone.

I returned to my mop and my corner in order to hide my traitorous face from her. One look and she'd have known I was concealing something. She said, "I was followed everywhere by a group of unemployed and unwashed cowboys, though I tried to lose them by dashing in and out of shops. They came nearly to the house before they finally wandered off. Poor Mrs. Babcockry is right that Bodie, with its fragments of humanity, has become no fit place to live."

To keep my back to Momma, I swished my mop to a corner I'd already cleaned. One more thing I hadn't mentioned — to keep from upsetting her — was about the guard of Horribles Papa had arranged for us. Had she known, she'd have indignantly sent them on their way. This secret made me smile, and hope, at the same time, that this unwashed group was keeping an eye on Ling Loi. But there was a strange and disturbing sensation within me — instead of being glad that Momma complained about Bodie, I was worried. For now the Horribles and their carefree madness called out to me. I longed for their camaraderie, their sophistication, their fearlessness. Rather than leave Bodie, now all I wanted was to stay.

Thursday, July 1, 1880
Dear Diary,

Eleanor has made a discovery! She asked me to come to her house after school and at first I made an excuse — it was indeed true — that I needed to go to the general store for mending thread, but the urgency of her request, and her promise that her father would not be at home, made me agree to it.

We passed a flock of wild sage grouse, all fat from late-spring gorging, and I wished I could trap or shoot some of them. They make for fine eating when browned in lard, though being small they are harder to pluck than ordinary chickens. Momma loves their livers mashed and mixed with onions and herbs, fried, and served on toast. However, it is a great test of skill to capture a sage grouse, as they scatter and fly low, and I am not up to the task. Once again I missed Papa, whose perfect aim would have guaranteed a fine meal.

"Do not look behind," Eleanor said to me as we watched the flock run in back of the apothecary. "Con Williams is following and I have no wish to speak with him."

"Oh, Eleanor, is he yet another beau of yours?" I whispered.

"He would like it to be so," she said, and grimaced. "But not I."

"But he's Teacher's brother," I teased. I knew Eleanor would not permit a person to court her just because it might give her an advantage with our teacher. She elbowed me in the side and shook her head.

By then Con had caught up with us. He apprenticed over at the livery, and was said to be a good hand with horses. Younger than Miss Williams, he shared her piercing voice and overall boniness. I had not seen him except in passing since he came to our home with a gun and a burning torch. "Miss Tucker, Miss Reddy," he said. "You are going the wrong direction! Back up Main Street, in the Occidental Hotel, the Horribles are rehearsing. They pulled the curtains but I can show you a way to listen to them."

"Please excuse us," Eleanor said curtly. "We have no wish to eavesdrop on the players and we are in somewhat of a hurry." She linked arms with me and continued walking briskly. I said nothing, for I have not yet told Ellie about my skit, as I wish to finish it first. I was curious, though, to see what satire the Horribles' *male* playwrights had produced.

"Ah, give it five minutes, Miss Tucker," Con

pleaded. "You should hear their little play about some of Bodie's biggest shareholders in the Standard Mine."

Eleanor stiffened, as certainly the skit was about her father and his friend Mr. McPhee, but she did not slacken her pace. Oh, I know what made Con beg: her delicate, fine-boned face with cupid's-bow lips and bright blue eyes, her graceful posture and upswept hair. She looked as if she belonged in an opera house, peering through a looking glass with a mother-of-pearl handle, not slogging through trash on a dirt street in a mining district. I figured Con just wanted to own all that beauty and be able to caress it whenever he pleased, clear and simple. She said, "I am weary of men hiding behind their masks."

Con must have been as let down as I was to hear this, but for different reasons, for he recoiled as if he'd been slapped. "Good-bye, Miss Tucker," he said, and turned his back. I heard the spatter of his saliva as it hit the dirt.

When we had come nearly to her house, I asked, "Eleanor, do you think Con Williams still plays at being a vigilante? Or were you really speaking of the Horribles?"

"Oh, no, I'm not weary of the Horribles," she said, and squeezed my hand. "I know you are drawn to them like a moth to a candle. They are filled with wit and insouciance, like you, and they seem to have such fun."

I did not know what *insouciance* meant, so I asked, hoping it was something good.

"Oh, lightsomeness. Con Williams is another matter. He has neither wit nor moral fiber that I've ever noticed; I believe he's an opportunist and a thief. As for the vigilantes — some would say that Mr. Babcockry got what he deserved, since he'd been a member himself, but Phillip Walheim was —" She broke off and I saw her eyes fill with tears.

It took me a second to realize she was talking about the family that had previously been driven from town. "You mean Mr. Walheim the boot maker? He was . . . ?"

"Not the boot maker. His son."

"Yes? His son . . . ?"

"Oh, Angie. I liked him. He read to me. Philosophy and theosophy. Books his grandfather sent him from back east. He had such a fine reading voice, and he could explain the most exotic theories of life and religion. And, and . . . oh, I don't know."

"I wish I had heard him!"

She looked both furious and sad at the same time. "He was the only boy who ever understood how much I want to go to St. Benedict's Academy in St. Joseph, Minnesota — how much I want to learn something useful. At the Academy they teach elocution, religion, logic, botany, bookkeeping, all the classical and womanly subjects, and, Angie, you can learn the piano, the organ, the harp, and the zither."

"How do you know so much about St. Benedict's?"

"We sent for the brochure. I know it by heart! But other boys ridicule the idea of a female having her own means of support, and my father . . . he gets angry and says he will never let me go far from him. Were it not for Miss Williams and her letters of introduction—"

"Miss Williams!" Ellie had shocked me several times in rapid succession.

"Oh, she is a terror with the paddle and dreadfully strict, but she has been a good friend to my mother." Ellie wiped her eyes with a frayed handkerchief, as if it was worn out from having wiped altogether too many tears. She added, "My mother could not have held up against my father were it not for the private encouragement of Miss Williams."

We had arrived at her house. "Now let us speak of this no longer," she said, with all the confidence and fortitude I was used to. "I will show you a secret. Prepare yourself if you can, Angie, for it is sure to shock you greatly."

Diary, what follows is the pitiable story. I shall keep you hidden, and should any soul be reading this without my knowledge, may you feel sorrow in your heart. Whether you can forgive as well as pity is for you to decide.

As she had promised, no one was at home. Eleanor bade me tie a kerchief over my hair, and doing the same, she took me to a shed behind the house. It had the musty smell of a windowless place seldom opened for airing, a resting place for deceased chairs and lifeless old tools. We stirred fine dust as we moved in the cramped, dark space.

Ellie opened a broken-down wooden ammunition box in a far corner. She lifted out a stack of brittle newspapers, a scrap of cloth with military medals pinned to it, a soldier's cap, a chipped mug. At the bottom lay a neat, flat bundle: layers of yellowed cotton cloth. Ellie brought it out of the trunk carefully and as she did a strong feeling of dread came over me; I wanted to run from the shed yet felt powerless to move. Frozen, I watched as she turned back the top layer of cotton fabric.

The tiny pair of red shoes and hooded red cape sent a shiver through me and prickled the back of my neck, despite the warm day. My hand trembled as I reached out to touch the leather and the soft wool. They were shrunken and stained and so small they made my heart catch.

"My father has hidden these clothes," Ellie whispered. "My mother never comes to this shed, and I'm certain she does not know about them — or if she does know, she cares not to be reminded. Why, Angie?" She looked searchingly into my eyes, as if she would find an answer there. "Does my father keep this secret out of shame? Out of fear?"

I gripped her shoulder. "Put them back, Ellie. This is not for us to question. I do not want to be here in this place any longer."

A fierce expression came upon her face, almost as if she had put on a mask — a mask of her own face, but carved with an expression of terrifying urgency. "But it is, Angie! It *is* for us to question, you and me. Why do you think the ghost child appeared to us in your father's antechamber? Because she cannot rest in peace — I'm certain of it. An injustice has been done and the child wants us to discover it. And somehow, you are the conduit."

"But why?"

She touched a row of miniature shoe buttons, one by one, as if they were a path she was following.

"Your father's study is a place where crimes are examined and justice is sought. The moment you brought me there, the ghost child . . . came to us, because—" She broke off.

"—because she wants us to learn the truth about her death." I finished.

She nodded.

"But what can we do? Show these clothes to your mother?"

"Oh, no, I think not that. I have a sense it would bruise her heart beyond repair."

My head must have disturbed a cobweb near the shed door. I brushed at it and just then a question came to me, like a spider that had been waiting there in hiding. "Ellie, how did you find out about this? How did you know to look inside the old box, and to dig under all the other things, and to pull back the layer of cotton?"

"You already know, Angie, don't you?" Her blue eyes burned through the dust-filled light from outside. "It was the ghost child. She led me here."

Sunday, July 4, 1880

Dear Diary,

Since today is Sunday, we Bodieites will celebrate our country's birthday tomorrow with many festivities including the Grand Fourth of July Ball. To get Eleanor away from the disturbing sadnesses in her house, I invited her to spend this afternoon with Momma and me. We aired our dresses and cleaned our shoes. We washed our hair and sat luxuriously in the sun until it dried. Momma discovered three gray hairs and rubbed into her roots a wash made of three drams of pure glycerin and four ounces of limewater. She said this helps prevent more gray hairs, which are an indication that the hair-producing organs are weakening. We teased her good-naturedly, as she looks young enough to be my sister and is often mistaken for such.

I pray that the ball will be festive. Just for that one day and night, I hope we will celebrate and dance with light hearts, leaving our many cares and worries out in the dusty street.

Tuesday, July 6, 1880

Dear Diary,

Yesterday's grand ball to celebrate Independence Day included startling surprises and revelations, a mystery solved, a standoff, an unmasking, an election, and almighty heroism. It will never be forgotten by any of us, for as long as we live, and this is not a schoolgirl exaggeration.

The Miners' Union Hall was patriotically decorated and crammed with us Bodieites as well as visitors from all over. It was smoky, stinky, loud, crowded, rowdy, hot, and magnificent. Ellie and I were having the most thrilling night of our lives!

We smiled when the widow Babcockry, resplendent in black mourning satin and trailed by many suitors, stopped to admire us. She said, "Oh, my heavens, you are the sun and the moon! How clever!" I wore a silver-gray dress with my white mask; Eleanor was in golden yellow, with a matching purse made from the same fabric. We fancied that I was mysterious, beguiling, and enchanting. She was aglow, brilliant, and fiery.

We'd embroidered moons on my bodice and suns on hers, using silver and gold silk thread.

Like all the women, Momma and Eleanor and I were in great demand as dance partners — not for any special talent but because there are ten males to every female in Bodie. The Horribles, disguised as devils and demons in red vests and horned masks, were the most persistent suitors. We danced for hours with an endless number of men, some in costume, some not — young, old, light-on-their-feet, and toe-stompers.

One dress stood out from all others and provoked a lively round of betting among the men — who also lined up to dance with her — as to the identity of its graceful wearer. It was a splendor of deep green silks, with ribbons all tiered and layered, showing a tiny waist and curves, yet not vulgar. Everyone watched when she danced, for the dress floated about her as if it were made from fragile dragonfly wings rather than fabric. The matching green silk mask, the sumptuous wig, the fine kid gloves, all indicated a woman of breeding and wealth. I will for the rest of my life desire to possess a dress exactly like that one, for I'm sure it would give me a magical, mysterious beauty that I otherwise completely lack.

It was no surprise, then, at midnight, when the Most Beautiful Costume Committee (none other than Mrs. Fahey, Mrs. McPhee, and Mrs. Rawbone) announced the winner of the blue ribbon. The lady's green silk shimmered as she curtsied; the room exploded with applause and shouts of "Who are you? Off with the mask!"

I heard a loud "Ha!" at the back of the room. I guessed who it was, even before he bounded to the platform and triumphantly removed his own and his wife's masks. The room erupted with cheers and whistles. Hats flew in the air.

Eli and Lottie Johl had been gone for nearly a week, and no one, it seems, had supposed they would return for the ball.

Meanwhile, I watched as the Most Beautiful Costume Committee conferred in a matronly little circle. Eleanor leaned in to whisper, "Angie, you don't think they'll change their minds, do you?" Her blue eyes threw sparks from behind her sun mask. I nodded. Yes, I was sure they would. Suddenly Momma appeared beside us with Mrs. O'Toole.

"They are *not* taking back that winning ribbon!" Sally O'Toole declared, shaking her head. Feathers from her mask and headdress became unglued and floated around us.

Momma agreed. "Just let them try!" she said.

Like me, Momma was wearing her best outfit. Hers was honey-colored linen to which we'd added delicate lace bands at the wrists and throat. Her mask, borrowed from Mrs. Babcockry, was rimmed in tiny pearls. Pink had returned to her cheeks, and except for the sad, missing-Papa look in her eyes, Momma was beautiful. I felt a thrill of pride when she and Sally O'Toole, arms linked and feathers wafting, marched over to stand with the Johls.

It was then that Mrs. Johl said she had an announcement. The room grew still, the musicians resting their instruments. Mrs. Johl said, "I danced with every man and boy in this room

tonight and I have the sore toes to prove it."
We all laughed. In a gesture both natural and
scandalous, both graceful and awkward, she
raised one foot and massaged the toe of her elegant
green silk shoe. The room watched, got a glimpse
of her slim, silk-encased ankle, and sighed. My
own toes ached in sympathy, but she was smiling and so was I. She steadied herself with a hand
on her husband's arm. "Anyway, I danced with
the three men who robbed us. I can identify them
even though they were wearing masks during the
robbery."

That brought a wave of murmurs. Eleanor
and I stood on tiptoe and peered around fancy
coiffures.

"Where's the sheriff?" someone shouted.

Another man answered, "Outside having
a snort. He took off the badge again tonight."

"But I'm wearing it now," a loud, insistent
voice called out. We all heard the distinctive
tapping of the sheriff's nail-studded boots, like
hammers pounding tin, as he made his way
across the room. "Far as that one dancing with

the highwaymen, it ain't possible. I arrested the mastermind of that robbery, Antoine Duval, this morning. He's in jail."

I felt such shock and confusion that at first I didn't notice when someone from the midst of a cluster of Horribles strode forward. He said conversationally, "Point of fact—Duval is not in jail. He's out on bail. I'm representing him as his lawyer."

He was wearing a serge suit, a red brocade vest, and a narrow black necktie. The legs of his trousers were tucked into polished black boots. The horns of his red mask curled inward. I recognized his faint, ironic smile, though not the waxed mustache and clean-shaven chin.

And even before I noticed his left sleeve, which was tucked into his belt, even before he whipped off his mask, I realized it was Papa.

Since I knew he hadn't been dead I wasn't too shocked, but some of the crowd like to die themselves at the sight of him, who they thought had been buried for some time now. They gasped as if from one huge throat, and a couple of women fainted and had to be caught before they dropped to the floor. Someone called, "Hey, it's Patrick Reddy, who got murdered a few weeks back! He's never missed a Bodie ball yet!"

I glanced at Momma, still standing with Mrs. O'Toole near the Johls. She grinned, acknowledging Papa's love of dramatic entrances; she didn't seem the least surprised to see him.

"Now, Mrs. Johl," Papa said smoothly, as if he were in court. "I'm sure we'd all like to know the identity of the actual robbers. Was this man one of them?" Papa gestured toward another devil-dressed Horrible, who was tall and lanky, with black hair curling at his neck and a spiked red tail. He removed his mask and faced Mrs. Johl. It was Antoine Duval.

Sheriff Pioche Kelley drew a large pistol and trained it on Papa. Everyone except Antoine moved back and away from the sheriff's line of fire.

Sheriff Kelley said, "You shoulda stayed dead, Reddy. This town was finally settling down, without you poking your nose into everything. Going behind my back to the judge in Bridgeport with his bail money. Givin' all the cutthroats and vermin free legal help. Hangin' around the jail to spy on me and Constable Kirgan." I began to understand why Papa had pretended to be dead. It gave everyone a chance to see how the sheriff would run things if no one stopped him. He rubbed a thumb across his badge, as if to polish it, and then continued telling Papa off.

"You been here five minutes and already ruined this ball. I want you out—out of here and out of Bodie. You got twenty-four hours, you and your family, to leave. Fair warning."

Papa laughed. Behind him, one of the Horribles performed a little pantomime. The gigantic tin sheriff's badge I'd seen before suddenly appeared on his chest. He puffed himself up and made his hands into guns, like kids do, "shooting" wildly. He "tripped" and turned a somersault, to wild applause.

The sheriff, however, was not amused. Papa remained silent, waiting for what the man would say next.

"This ain't no courtroom. You can't conduct

no legal matters in the Miners' Union Hall." The sheriff didn't have a big voice like Papa, but one he had to push at you like a punch.

Papa replied in a mild way, "That's like saying you can only pray in church."

The sheriff looked like he was trying to figure that out. Several people around me laughed, which seemed to infuriate him. "I'm taking my prisoner back to jail," he announced. "I ain't seen no papers on him and it's plain he escaped. He figured I'm about to arrest his cohorts in the Johl robbery. The three of them loose" — the sheriff shook his head at the thought of this imminent danger — "means decent citizens could get murdered in their beds, children kidnapped, horses stolen, and every saloon in Bodie robbed."

"You forgot to mention tracking dirt in on the rug," Antoine Duval said in his growly-bear way.

When the laughter died down a bit, Mr. Ward waved an arm in the air. He was dressed as an undertaker and wore no mask, a costume that must be admired for its simplicity if not imagination. "Tracking in dirt, yes," he said, staring hard at the sheriff. "Dirt." He let the word hang there a moment. "But escaping?" He shook his mournful head.

"Such logic escapes me," Antoine agreed. "No sense to it, nor dollars, either."

Mr. Ward added, "I say let Mrs. Johl tell her story, and let *us* get back to our ball."

The sheriff ignored Mr. Ward, threw Antoine a threatening look, and motioned with his pistol. "Get back, Reddy. I don't want to have to shoot you 'cause you're interferin' with the duties of a sworn officer."

Papa did not move aside as ordered. Just then a girl I took to be one of the Higgins sisters darted in front of the crowd, skipped past the sheriff, and, with her back to him, curtsied before Antoine. "Won't you please dance with me, Mr. Antoine?" she asked sweetly.

Everyone laughed nervously. With the whiskey-reeking sheriff waving his pistol and shouting threats, I decided she must be either very brave or very foolish. Mr. Duval bowed, kissed her forehead, and said, "*Chérie*, there's not a thing I'd love better. Why don't you go ask the fiddler to play us a waltz?" As she flounced off toward the musicians, I admired her light blue satin dress with its little apron and matching mask. Her hair had been done up in a chignon and was covered with a blue tulle net, and I could not tell which sister it was.

By custom and agreement, none of the men had brought their firearms to the ball (except, of course, the sheriff) but suddenly Antoine's outstretched hand held a tiny handgun. He pointed it at the sheriff. The derringer was all but swallowed by his hand, yet his intention was clear.

Sheriff Kelley swore violently and then said, "Put the derringer down, Duval."

"Certainly," Antoine answered. "Right after I lodge its bullet in your miserable excuse for a heart."

I am sure, dear diary, that no one there doubted he would do it, or that he could.

I watched as a man with shoulder-length straw-colored hair and a big porous nose made his way through the crowd. He jammed a Stetson onto the back of his head and elbowed his way toward the door.

Papa looked up. "Oh, Constable Kirgan, would you mind waiting just a moment or two? Gentlemen, would you secure the door, please?" Several "demons"—big ones—formed a human barrier in front of the door and a wedge around the constable.

Mr. Kirgan locked eyes with Papa. His voice was tense and hard. "I need to get to the jail right now, Reddy."

"Ah, another escapee requiring your presence this time?"

Everyone laughed, and Mr. Ward said, "Stick around a while, Constable. It is we who require your presence."

A piercing scream interrupted this stalemate. It was the girl in the blue dress, now with her arms being twisted behind her back by Con Williams, who wore no mask. "She snuck him the gun!" he shouted. "I saw it—she had it under her apron!" He pulled the silk cord of her mask, which fell off to reveal not the Higgins sister I'd expected, but Ling Loi.

Con Williams spat on the floor. (This man poses a challenge to my faithful recording of events, as his speech is littered with the most appalling language. I shall indicate the intent of his words, dear diary, rather than the words themselves.) He said, "What the (foul-mouthed noun) is this (rude adjective) China girl doing at the ball? Who let her in?" Tears came to my eyes. I felt so many things: joy at seeing her again, exasperation at her foolhardy actions, fury at Con, and swooning admiration for her courage. Eleanor grabbed my arm as I started forward, saying, "Angie! Don't become another target! It won't help your father or Antoine if you do that!" Of course she was right.

Con Williams shouted, "Drop the derringer or I'll (uncouth adverb) break both her arms, Duval."

Someone in the crowd roared, "Take it outside! Leave the women and children out of it!"

And then came the earsplitting voice of Miss Williams: "Con! You let that child go, right now! You are behaving disgracefully and shamefully!"

Miss Williams, costumed as a nun from the Middle Ages with an elaborate starched wimple, began to advance on her brother and I *almost* felt sorry for him. I knew that after his sister got done with him he would regret playing the big brave vigilante who savaged little girls.

I glanced at Momma, still standing by the Johls. Though the situation was horribly tense, she looked almost serene; she had every confidence that Papa would handle it. I, myself, was desperate with worry. The sheriff and the constable were angry and shamed and desperate, and whatever their plan was, if they had a plan, it was not going well.

"Now," the sheriff said, striding quickly behind Momma so that she was between him and Antoine, "the next thing that happens concerns Mrs. Reddy" — he swung his pistol so that it pointed at Momma — "one minute she's a widow, the next minute she's *not* a widow, and the *next* minute her *husband's* a widower. I mean it, Reddy — and you, too, Duval — drop the derringer or I'll shoot her." But his hands were shaking and his voice was strangled.

"I'm unarmed," Papa said, walking deliberately to the sheriff's side, "as well as one-armed. Not exactly an army." But the sheriff wasn't distracted by my father's little joke. He cocked, pointed, and was pulling the trigger to kill Momma, when Papa reached out and thrust his one and only thumb between the hammer and cartridge, which prevented the gun from going off. He wrenched it out of the sheriff's grasp and kicked him between the legs. The officer doubled over and fell, groaning, to the floor.

Momma flew to Papa, grabbed his face, and kissed him full on the mouth. She quickly bandaged his bleeding thumb with a handkerchief and then kissed him again, as if the whole town of Bodie weren't watching — and clapping! How glad I was for my mask!

After a moment, Papa waved his hand above his head, Momma's handkerchief like a delicate white flag, and the clapping died down. He said, "Looks like Bodie's arm of the law suffered a setback today."

The Chairman of the Ball, Herbert McPhee,

pounded the floor with his gold-handled cane. "All right, Reddy," he said in a commanding voice. "Enough theatrics. I'll see these men get thrown out and we'll discuss it later. Let's resume the ball with some civility."

Thrown out! The sheriff had almost killed Momma! I glared at Mr. McPhee's soft face and opaque eyes.

But Papa wasn't finished. "Certainly," he said, "but before we do, there are a couple more legal matters that need settling. They concern you personally, McPhee. The unsolved crime of the Johl robbery." He turned to me. "My daughter has something that may help us solve it. Angel, please give me the envelope I asked you to bring."

I went to Papa and drew the envelope from my purse, the one marked "601" and sealed with wax.

"601," Papa said, holding it up to display the boldly written numbers. "The secret group of citizens that is trying to run this town. I was told that this is a list of names. I have not broken the seal so I don't know who is included."

Eleanor's father, Mr. Tucker, spoke up. He had been standing quietly with Mr. McPhee and a few other of the town's most wealthy men. He said, "Anyone can write names on a piece of paper. Doesn't prove anything."

Papa smiled. "I've been assured that this list contains signatures of the members. In their own handwriting." The envelope seemed to cause considerable agitation in the room. Several men took a nip from their pocket flasks. Many of the wives cast worried glances at their husbands.

Someone in the crowd shouted, "Let's get on with it! Where did you get that envelope, Reddy?"

"It was given to me for safekeeping," Papa said, "by a friend of someone very close to one of the signers. This person is not proud of what the vigilantes have done and what they intend to do."

Suddenly I knew something that I hadn't known I'd known. I turned to Eleanor, who was listening to Papa. "You?" I whispered. She nodded imperceptibly, then leaned close and spoke in my ear.

"I took it from my father's desk and gave it to

Miss Williams, who gave it to your father. Untie my ribbon, will you?" Freed from her mask, she wore an expression of both anguish and hope on her face. "Even though my own father is involved with them, I hate the 601 vigilantes, Angie. They're like mean, greedy little boys allowed to run wild."

Papa turned his back on the sheriff and spoke again to the ball chairman. Mr. McPhee had a large head with a fat, round face resting on a tough, wiry body, like a half man, half baby. "Now, Mr. McPhee, I understand you know everything that happens in this town, often *before* it happens. Perhaps you would like to tell us who was responsible for the Johl robbery."

Everyone knows Mr. McPhee is one of the largest shareholders in the Standard Mine, and the richest man in Bodie. I guess he was not used to taking suggestions from others. "That had nothing to do with the 601. It was just a robbery and no one is going to believe that woman can identify masked bandits. Give me the list, Reddy," he ordered.

"Who are you trying to protect, McPhee?

Yourself?" When Mr. McPhee only glared through narrowed eyes, Papa slapped the envelope against his leg. "Here's our offer: This unopened envelope will be locked in the Wells Fargo safe. It will remain unopened until there is another incident of vigilantism — until the 601 try again to take the law into their own hands. In exchange, Wells Fargo agent Mr. Antoine Duval wants the names of the three men who robbed the Johls and your assurance that their money will be returned."

Mr. McPhee laughed. "Well, let Mr. Antoine Duval find out who they are for himself."

The devil who still held the tiny derringer said, "I already have. We know who they are, and we have abundant evidence, including Mrs. Johl's observations about the hole she shot with this derringer in the hat of one, the bite marks her dog left in the boot of another, and her own ring on the finger of the third." A roar of comments spread through the room and then everyone quieted when Antoine continued.

"You are right that the robbers are not directly connected with the vigilantes. They will be tried in a court of law. But the deal Mr. Reddy is representing will allow the good people of Bodie to see tonight the corruption that's going on, and a big part of that, McPhee, is your tolerance of it."

Mr. McPhee examined the jeweled collar of his cane. I saw his jaw clench and unclench. "No deal," he said to Antoine.

A tiny, tidy, graying woman rushed to his side. It was Mrs. McPhee, still clutching the Best Costume blue ribbon. She looked irritable, as if someone had wiped his dirty hands on her best tablecloth. She said, "Oh, Herbert, do as they say. Everyone knows Con Williams was involved, and for Heaven's sake he's wearing the stolen emerald ring on his pinky right now!"

People standing near Con Williams moved away as Antoine covered him with the derringer. The sheriff cursed from his place on the floor. But it was the voice of Miss Williams that rang out as she once again advanced on her brother reprovingly. "Stop trying to get it off!" she said. "It's quite obviously too tight!" Con rammed his hand into his pocket and pulled his hat down low over his eyes. Many of us laughed at his discomfort, for we knew his sister was a force to be reckoned with.

Mrs. McPhee was not finished with her husband. "Now will you kindly promise that the Johls' money will be returned and give Mr. Duval and Mr. Reddy the names of the other two highwaymen so we can get back to our ball?"

Much more slowly, Mr. McPhee turned his imposing eyes to his wife. I had seen him castigate men who got in his way on the street, flailing at them with his cane. He was rumored to be an excellent shot with either rifle or revolver. But now he seemed like a boy caught stealing marbles — yet not quite ready to fess up.

"First give Mrs. Johl her ribbon," he said to Mrs. McPhee. "She deserves it."

"Oh, all right!" Mrs. McPhee huffed.

She marched over to Mrs. Johl, who said, "Hello, Mrs. McPhee. It's nice to meet you . . . finally." For a few moments nothing happened, and I think Ellie and I were holding our breath.

Mrs. McPhee looked alert and a little surprised. Then she reached up and pinned the ribbon on

Mrs. Johl's dress. "Herbert is right," she said. "You deserve this. And the next time you and your husband visit Bodie, you must come to tea."

"In truth, what I should really like," Lottie Johl said, "is to come back and serve on the Committee of Arrangements for the Fourth of July Ball and Parade next year."

"Done," said Mrs. McPhee, and nodded to her husband.

"The highwaymen were Kelley and Kirgan," said Mr. McPhee, and nodded to Antoine.

"Done," said Antoine, and nodded to the Horribles on either side of the sheriff and the constable.

"Done," shouted those men, and they restrained the two officers of the law who had, along with Con Williams, robbed the Johls.

The banjo player strummed a chord. The fiddler lifted his bow. A newly masked devil was suddenly standing by my side. "Will the brightest moon that ever shone in Bodie favor me with a dance?" he asked.

"Done," I said to Antoine Duval.

Later

The grand ball ended at dawn. The morning-shift miners, deep inside our mountain digging gold from its veins, never discovered the gold spilled on its crest by the rising sun. "How fleeting," I said to Ellie with a great sigh as we walked home, "are the most dazzling of riches."

Eleanor, mask and purse dangling from one hand, glowed with an inner light. We both had sore feet, dark smudges beneath our eyes, and a thrilling desire, already, for the next ball — though it would not be for months.

After the sheriff and constable and Con Williams were taken away — Papa gracefully declined each one's request to serve as his lawyer — a quick election for a provisional sheriff was held. Mr. Ward was elected and he mournfully accepted with the stipulation that someone look after his shop during his absences. Hank Babcockry volunteered for this job and was signed on. Teamster Zachariah Gibson and carpenter Silus Smith, both boarders at Mrs. O'Toole's, were appointed as temporary deputies.

My parents had walked home at around midnight but they'd allowed me to stay until the end. Antoine Duval was escorting the three of us — Eleanor, her mother, and me — to our homes. Along Main Street, a light shone in the rear of Ward's Furniture and Undertaking. "Let's go 'round to the back," Ellie said. "I think I know who's there."

Mrs. Tucker was indignant. "Eleanor! I won't hear of it! That is where Mr. Ward does his embalming and keeps his caskets."

"Dear Mother," Eleanor said, "come with me for a moment. There is something we need to see." She linked arms with her mother and gave me a pleading look until I took Mrs. Tucker's other arm. I said, "Mrs. Tucker, I believe Mr. Ward is a great friend — of Bodie and of us. I think he has been watching over us and protecting us. He will not mind if we go inside, I am certain."

She became resigned and gave no further protest, but I myself was secretly reluctant to revisit the musty, strong-smelling little room yet again.

But Eleanor's insistence on taking us there inspired my tired feet.

Mr. Ward was standing in the alley by his back door. "Ah," he said, "how unusual, yet fortuitous. He, that is, Mr. Tucker, has been searching for something, muttering and crying. Muttering, yes, and crying. Quite in a bad state, Mr. Tucker. Won't you go in?"

"I'll be waiting for you here," Antoine said to me in a low tone. He and Mr. Ward began discussing the events of the evening, leaning against the back alley wall as we went inside.

Mr. Tucker was sitting on the sawdust-covered floor, motionless in the half-light, as if he'd lost his way and was trying to get his bearings. When he saw us he began scooting backward toward the curtain that led to the front room. I stayed by the door.

"Wait, Father!" Ellie said. "I have something you lost! It was sent by someone you loved, when you still knew how to love."

Mr. Tucker had aged as if the long night were ten thousand nights, turning him into a very old man. He fixed vacant eyes on Eleanor's purse as she opened it. When she laid a pair of tiny red shoes and a small red cape on the floor beside him, he began to tremble violently. He wrapped his arms around his knees and rocked himself side to side. "No, no, no, please, no," he pleaded.

"Explain what happened, Father," Eleanor said quietly. "Tell us now."

Mrs. Tucker pushed past me to stand with Ellie, their arms around each other's waists. She had not worn a mask to the ball, but her face was now like a frozen mask. She gazed at the clothes and her expression grew puzzled, then comprehending, then stricken. She cried, "Oh, my God! Dear God!"

Mr. Tucker's face seemed to crumple. "You had almost died, my Ida," he said in a pleading tone. "Fifteen years ago, it was, we had that little place in Aurora. The midwife saved your life, and new baby Eleanor's, too." He glanced toward Ellie, but quickly looked away as if seeing her blinded him. He turned his piteous eyes back to his wife. "But she had another birthing to attend. She gave our girl Hope a corn-husk dolly and then she left. When you and the infant finally slept, I packed my hunting gear — it was rabbits I wanted. They were for you, Ida, to bring some home for supper. Little Hope wanted to go with me — it was spring, you remember, Ida, and the winter had been almighty hard, and she'd been cooped up so long. So I dressed her . . ." He broke off, heaving a great sob that made me bow my head in pity.

I had no idea what he had done, but I did know he had suffered from it horribly.

"I dressed her and wrapped her in that red cape, so if there were other hunters they wouldn't mistake her for a little animal. That was right, wasn't it, Ida? I slipped her feet into her . . . her red shoes; fastened each button." He wiped his nose and eyes on his sleeve, and seemed unaware that he continued to cry. I felt my heart pounding as I listened. No other sound interrupted as Mr. Tucker continued from his position on the floor. The bald spot on the top of his head seemed like a raw pink wound.

"I carried Hope and my gear to a little

melting-snow stream in that canyon beyond the house, and when she squirmed, I let her down so gentle, and showed her to be quiet, and she understood, Ida. She knew not to scare the rabbits; she was real smart for such a tiny one, only six months over a year in age."

Mr. Tucker looked into a distance only he could see, his eyes glazed and his voice trancelike. "You have to look for shapes, not color or movement. Rabbits knew I was there. They made themselves invisible, freezing in place the way they do, looking at you with only one of their eyes so they blend into the ground and the rocks and shadows. You have to know how to search for them, search for the round shape of the haunch, the long up-down line of their ears.

"Hope didn't pay attention; she wanted to gather up sticks for her new dolly, I guess, making little piles of them, so I walked on farther into the canyon, knew I'd find rabbits there like I'd done before.

"And, Ida, I swear, I was thinking of you, and how glad you'd be when I came home with fresh meat, and then I spotted them. A good distance apart so it wouldn't be easy, but I believed I could do it. They were foraging and they knew I was there. I had to wait, that's all, that's what every hunter knows: You have to be patient. Once they moved closer together I might could kill them both.

"I waited, waited, thought about the supper we'd have that night, waited. Didn't even bother with the cramps in my legs, didn't move, hardly breathed, and finally they each took little hops closer together, just like I wanted. I squeezed off a shot and then another, but only winged the second rabbit.

"'Course I followed its bloody trail; you can't leave an animal to die like that. I wanted that meat for us, Ida. And the fur skins, I was thinking we could trade or sell 'em—we needed money and goods. That's why I did it, Ida, for you. Later there was money, more and more of it, but back then . . . I killed the second rabbit and bagged them and I was proud and wanted to show you right away—thinking how pleased you'd be. I was planning how I'd skin them first, then bring them to you in your stew pot.

"Maybe even stop first at Old Man Reid's, get him to lend us some salt pork and onions in exchange for a rabbit pie later. You know, I thought you could stuff and roast one of them and stew the other for rabbit pies. I could almost taste your pies."

Mr. Tucker was silent then for some time. He continued to weep. Then he tried to look again into Ellie's eyes but I saw him flinch—he couldn't do it. He gazed down at his own shaking hands and continued. "I was nearly home; close enough to see you through the window, holding the newborn and watching, and then your face changed, Ida, and you looked as if God himself had thumped you. That's when I come to realize I'd made it all the way back without Hope.

"I couldn't tell you." He shook his head from side to side. "I had to make a different story than what happened. I *had* to. I says to you, 'Ida, what is the matter? What is so wrong?' You come out and peered all around me and you says, 'Hope!

Where is she? You were gone so long and I woke and could not find her!'

"So I look at you and I know you'll kill me if I tell the truth, I know sure as God that you'll kill me. So I says, 'You let her wander off? Ida, what have you done?' Then I say, 'No, you stay here. I'll find Hope. But,' I says—and may God forgive me, Ida—I says to you, 'remember that you are the mother.'"

His voice broke and for a while he sobbed uncontrollably, rocking himself.

In a cold, commanding voice, Eleanor said, "Finish the story, Father."

He nodded. After a moment he said, "I threw the rabbits on the step. My blood was cold in my veins, Ida, but I had to do it. I said, 'You must take better care of the children. I cannot provide food and shelter and protection *and* be the nursemaid.' You see, Ida, I had to show I was the man of the family. You see, don't you? You had to understand it wasn't my fault what happened."

He took a deep, shuddering breath. "I went back, calling and calling, but she didn't answer. I found her facedown in a puddle. I gathered her little wet body to me and held her and held her, and I swear if I could have brought her back to life by giving my own I would of done it, Ida. I'd lost one daughter and gained another on the same day, and I . . . I made you believe that you were the cause of both, the birth and the death. I had to hide the red clothes, to make it like she wandered off on her own when you wasn't looking — she was too young to have dressed herself. I thought what I did was God's will, Ida."

Mrs. Tucker stood quietly staring down at her husband. Her face was expressionless but her eyes, the same beautiful blue as Eleanor's, seemed as if they could pierce him.

"Go on, Father," Eleanor said. "Tell us what you did next."

He took something from his pocket and shot a glance at me by the door. His eyes were like dark stones. I was surprised he even realized I was in the room. "Make her leave," Mr. Tucker said, trying for command in his voice, trying for his usual authority.

But Eleanor was, now, the stronger of them. "No," she said. We all waited. He shook his hand, making a clicking sound that filled the room. Finally he continued.

"All I knew was I had to hide the cape and the shoes. Had to do it. Then I saw two hunters comin' upstream. They hadn't seen me. I couldn't let them find out what I was doing. So then I knew I'd have to scare them away. If I didn't, everything would go wrong, see?

"I aimed and hit one of 'em in the arm. The other starts shouting for me to throw down the gun but I don't because I still have to make them leave. But that second fella he sees me and shoots and I feel a sting like a bee at the side of my ear and I know the next shot he won't miss, so I throw in my gun and clamber away from Hope and the clothes. Got my hands in the air, say it's an accident. The man I shot is bleeding bad so we make a tourniquet and carry him over to town. He's big, and if I hadn't a helped he'd a died one way or the other.

"Then I went back for Hope. Was afraid to bury the clothes, afraid they'd turn up; knew it was a bad plan. So I kept them in my kit and later hid them in a trunk. That's all, Ida. We buried Hope the next day in the Aurora cemetery. You see, I did what I had to do. Didn't have a choice."

It was quiet in the embalming room, except for the clicking. He opened his hand, palm flat, and we all looked down at the gold dice, shining in the gloom.

Ellie said, "But Hope thinks you *did* have a choice, Father. Isn't that right?"

He rolled the dice between his palms. "I gambled and lost," he said. With great force he threw the dice into a dark corner. He reached toward one small shoe, then withdrew his hand quickly, as if his fingertips had been burned. "Hope keeps coming back, Ellie, haunting me. She . . . wants me. I can't bear up under it any longer. I'm going mad. I've gone mad. Please make her leave me alone, now I've confessed. Make her go away, Ida! Please!"

I believe that Eleanor became a woman that night, in the sense of having grown to a maturity of mind and feelings, of crossing some bridge only to discover that evil and deception exist at the other side, even in the heart of one you love. She learned that her father had caused a death and blamed it on his blameless wife; she learned how he'd taken my father's arm. And so she was forced to see the true depths of his weak and tortured soul. She blazed with twisted twin flames of fury and of pity.

Her mother remained silent and seemed unhearing. Finally Ellie spoke. "You will purchase this coffin from Mr. Ward," she said, choosing the smallest of the boxes in a stack behind her father. She opened the lid; it was just large enough. With great care and tenderness, she laid the cape and shoes inside.

"It is over now, Father," she said, and closed the lid. She handed it to him. "Hope wants you to go to Aurora and bury this alongside her body. May God have mercy on you."

Eleanor took Mrs. Tucker's hand and held it

to her cheek. She said, "Mother," and she whispered that one word so tenderly it filled my eyes with tears.

Mr. Tucker, groaning, seemed to summon all his strength just to get to his feet. The tiny coffin appeared to overwhelm him with its weight. He looked at his wife, daughter, and all around the dusty, silent room. None of us returned his gaze. It was as if he did not exist. We left him standing there with Hope's last wish.

In the cool, rosy morning outside, I should not have been surprised to find Ling Loi in the alley with Mr. Ward and Antoine—she who appears and disappears like a magician's apprentice. But the beautiful light blue silk gown, the mask and chignon, had been replaced by her usual cotton pants and jacket, long braid, and serious, unsmiling countenance. She stood beside Miss Williams, who was also back to her old self, no longer a nun from the Middle Ages but terrifying all the same.

I pulled Ling Loi aside. "Where's your dress?" I asked. "It was so pretty."

She scowled at me. "Lottle gave it to me and I still have it. But this is who I am. Chinese, remember?"

"Oh, I'd completely forgotten," I said sarcastically. "*Yes*, I remember." Then I realized something. "You were the 'boy' who stowed away in the Johls' wagon, weren't you? And at the ball it was Mrs. Johl who gave you the derringer you passed to Antoine."

"It was your idea—well, stowing away was."

"What? *My* idea?"

"One time you asked me if I would ever stow away to China. Bridgeport is much closer than China and it was all I could think to do."

"So you've been with the Johls all this time?"

"No. And stop trying to know everything about my life."

"Ling Loi, you're so stubborn! I missed you, is all."

"Not enough to find me." She pinned me with her eyes in that way she has where it feels like you're looking into a gun barrel and you hope she won't decide to fire.

"In Bridgeport? How would I do that?"

"No, in Bodie. Miss Williams came and found me along the road after she read the newspaper story about the stowaway. I lived with her while we decided what to do. And," she leaned in to whisper, "don't *ever* say anything bad about Miss Williams again."

"I won't. Except—"

"Angie, never, *ever*."

Slowly and clearly, I said, "I am trying to call a truce. Okay?"

Slowly and clearly, she said, "Were we fighting?"

I laughed. "We Irish are always fighting—didn't you know?"

And then a fine and rare thing happened. Ling Loi laughed, too.

"I've made the arrangements," Teacher screeched, and those words somehow magically transformed Mrs. Tucker's face from melancholic to elated.

Miss Williams continued in her brisk way. "I will be the girls' chaperone on the afternoon stage next Monday. Everything has been set for Ling Loi. The good sisters of St. Benedict's are eager to educate a Chinese girl in church history and in every particular. She will do quite well, I'm entirely certain. Mr. and Mrs. Johl are sponsoring her and they repaid her parents' debt to Mr. Chung. Though at first most reluctant to let her go, he and Popo finally gave their blessing."

Eleanor shouted, "Mother! Does this mean that I shall go to Minnesota? To St. Benedict's Academy? Why have you not told me?" She hugged her mother so fiercely I thought Mrs. Tucker might faint.

"Once more unto the breach," I thought, as in my chest an ache suddenly lodged, a jealous bitter realization that Eleanor and Ling Loi would be together someplace very far from me. Though I had no wish to leave Papa and Momma, I envied my friends in my lonely, dark heart.

My face must have registered shock and anguish, for Eleanor said, "Oh, Angie, please don't look so . . . so miserable! It's really the most wonderful thing — Miss Williams has written countless letters to the school —" She turned to our teacher. "I can never repay your kindness, Miss Williams! St. Benedict's Academy is what I've always wanted!"

The only good part that I could find in this news was the departure of Miss Williams. As if she had heard my thoughts, Mrs. Tucker said, "Miss Williams will be attending a teacher college in order to learn the newest, most modern education methods and practices. She will be nearby, and she will help should you girls encounter any problem." I sincerely hoped (but did not say aloud) that those methods and practices Miss Williams would be studying would not include the paddle.

Then I remembered, finally, a shred of manners, and offered Ellie and Ling Loi all my best wishes.

Eleanor said, "I will write to you every week, and you must do the same, Angie. You see Bodie in a way no one else does, right through and clear-eyed. I shall depend on you for a faithful account of all the news and events." She gave me a private look that meant I should share, especially, any "news and events" of a romantic nature. I promised her I would.

If Mrs. Tucker's husband had aged dramatically inside Mr. Ward's shop, she, by contrast, looked more youthful — like a shorter, rounder, softer version of Ellie. She took my hand. "I will be the provisional teacher here, until they can find another woman willing to come to Bodie. You'll be a fine help to me, Angie." I was pleased that Mrs. Tucker thought she could rely on me, and thus I determined to do my best.

A hand rested on my shoulder — from the corner of my eye I saw clean nails on the long, ink-stained fingers of a bank clerk–detective–actor. I turned to him.

He said, "We have a Horrible offer for you."

"Would that involve ink stains on my fingers? I'm not Swift, you know."

"But you *are* quick. The vote was unanimous."

So I was to be a playwright, news that made

my breath catch in my throat with the glory of it. By day I would teach, and by night, with Mr. Swift and Mr. Shakespeare for company, I would use my pen to feed tragic and comic words into the mouths of my players. I would find stories in Bodie's best nuggets—in secrets behind masks.

"There's something else," Antoine said in my ear. "I've made a discovery."

I hadn't realized he pursued mining interests, and stared at him in astonishment. I whispered, "A vein?"

"A larger discovery—a major lode—the greatest treasure in Bodie. I shall have to hurry to stake my claim and register it properly."

I did not respond, feeling a keen and unwarranted disappointment. I should have been glad for his fortune, though I'd learned that mining brought bad luck as often as good. I frowned hard at him for not having figured this out, too.

He laughed and said, "What I've discovered is a cure much sweeter than Swift's for hearts injured by indignation."

Confused, I asked, "Gold?"

He shook his head and, in one word — made to shine by his way of saying it — he answered, "You." He'd earned an almighty smile for that, and he got one.

Sometimes a casket can be full of both trouble and hope. *I* was full of the certainty that with diligence, I could make time, every day, for a player and for plays. Trouble and hope suited me fine, and might even turn out Horribly wonderful.

Epilogue

In 1881, as Bodie's boom continued to decline, Angie and her parents moved to San Francisco. Patrick Reddy reestablished his law practice and maintained his long streak of never losing a case. Angie worked for her father and spent all the money she earned attending plays and theatrical shows of every sort. She continued keeping a diary. By the time she entered the University of California at Berkeley, she had written and published a five-act play based on her experiences as a young teenager during Bodie's gold rush. The play enjoyed a long run at major venues throughout the country and made Angie's reputation (writing under the name A. M. Reddy) as a playwright.

In the aftermath of the devastating 1906 earthquake, at the age of fifty-seven, Emma Reddy worked tirelessly to help and nurse those injured in the quake. She died from exhaustion and pneumonia as a result of these efforts.

Ling Loi Wing and Eleanor Tucker graduated from St. Benedict's Academy in St. Joseph. Eleanor married a railroad magnate and became a philanthropist, endowing colleges and other schools for women. Ling Loi made her way to the Kingdom of Hawai'i, where she remained the rest of her long life. She married and bore five sons and many of her descendants still populate the islands. Angie, Eleanor, and Ling Loi corresponded with one another throughout their lives, though they never met again.

Sheriff Pioche Kelley, Constable Kirgan, and Con Williams were convicted of numerous crimes. They were held in the jail adjoining the warden's house in Bridgeport. The jail shared a wall with the parlor of the house, where the warden's daughter often played the piano. When she did, the prisoners sang along in top voice, which encouraged her to bang the keys even harder. At the same time, under cover of the noise, they sawed the bars of their prison. Eventually they escaped. Their whereabouts were never discovered.

Miss Williams returned to Bodie. Big Bill Monahan met the stage and carried her bags. He succeeded in making her knees, elbows, and attitude considerably less sharp by feeding her custard pie and molasses pudding. They eloped and relocated to a frontier town called Los Angeles, where the weather was temperate.

Hank Babcockry became a respected lawman. He wore suspenders for the rest of his life.

Lottie Johl was not able to serve on the Committee of Arrangements for the 1881 Fourth of July Ball. She died in March of that year as a result of an incorrectly filled prescription for medicine. Eli Johl insisted she be buried in the consecrated ground of the Bodie cemetery, and the townsfolk, still intolerant of her past and after much controversy, finally agreed, as long as her grave was close to the fence. Eli decorated her grave with infinite, lavish care and spent many hours there over the years, grieving.

Antoine Duval continued working for several years as a detective for Wells Fargo & Co. He pursued some of the most hardened criminals throughout the West, bringing most of them into custody. While recuperating from a gunshot wound to his shoulder, Antoine attended a showing of *The Bold Bad Boys of Bodie* in San Francisco. At the end of the play he went backstage and, in view of the entire troupe of actors and stagehands, proposed on bended knee to the playwright. Angie said, "Are you afraid?" to which Antoine replied, "Yes, afraid you will refuse; how did you know?" She said, "Because 'boldness is a mask for fear, however great.'" She liked his boldness, his wit, his insouciance, and his tragic eyebrow, as she always had and as she always would, so she accepted.

Life in America
in 1880

Historical Note

The town of Bodie did not exist before gold was discovered nearby in 1859. At an elevation of 8,375 feet, on the windswept and rocky eastern side of the Sierra, the weather is dramatic and extreme in every season.

At that time, the Kuzedika, a specific group of the Mono Paiute Native Americans, were the people living in what is now the Mono County region (not in the Bodie area itself) when W. S. Bodie (or "Bodey" or "Body") and the gold-seekers arrived. The harsh, dry landscape required great skill and many strategies for survival: hunting, gathering, some agriculture, and trading. Kuzedika settlements in the area had dwindled by 1880 because of land encroachment by European Americans and the resultant disruption of the local ecosystem. Settlers, miners, and merchants greatly diminished the plants and animals on which the

Kuzedika depended for survival. Like the Chinese, Kuzedika people in Bodie lived in their own section of town.

The Chinese community in Bodie numbered some 350 residents according to the 1880 census report. No Chinese children were listed. At the time of this story, the Chinese were not eligible for membership in the Bodie Miners' Union. Two years later, the Chinese Exclusion Act, a way of eliminating job competition from Chinese labor, was enacted. This marked the first time in American history that members of a specific ethnic group were denied entry and naturalization rights on the basis of race. It was not repealed until sixty-one years later, in 1943.

The National Park Service website includes an article on the history of Chinese Americans in California with a description of the Bodie Chinese American community in 1880: www.nps.gov/history/history/online_books/5views/5views3e.htm.

Many of the characters in *Behind the Masks* were real people, and all the saloons, businesses, streets, the cemetery, the Chinese quarter, the

Reddy home, and the Miners' Union Hall existed in Bodie in 1880. Some of them are still standing, although a few have moved. According to "Map of Bodie, Mono Co., California, 1880" (c. 1991 Brownell Merrell) compiled from period sources and made available by the California Department of Parks and Recreation at Bodie Historic Park, the jail in that year was located, as stated in the story, at the *end* of Bonanza Street. By the following year a new, larger jail had been built at the beginning of Bonanza Street, where it appears on contemporary maps of the town.

Brothers Ned and Patrick Reddy were extremely famous in their day. Patrick lost his arm in a gunfight and took up the study of law at the urging of his nurse, Emma, whom he later married. He was a brilliant courtroom lawyer and at one point had law offices in both Bodie and San Francisco. The Reddy house remains intact in Bodie. Robert P. Palazzo's "The Fighting Reddy Brothers" in *The Album: Times and Tales of Inyo-Mono*, Chalfant Press, 1996, provides a finely researched portrait.

Patrick and Emma Reddy did not have children; Angeline is entirely fictional.

Eli and Lottie Johl were well-known residents of Bodie, and Lottie's background and subsequent rejection by the "respectable" women in town is essentially as presented in the novel. A piece of her artwork is displayed in the Bodie Museum (the former Miners' Union Hall). Marguerite Sprague's *Bodie's Gold: Tall Tales & True History from a California Mining Town*, University of Nevada Press, 2003, documents in detail the Johls' story while providing a comprehensive view of life in Bodie. The name of the establishment where Lottie worked prior to her marriage to Eli is difficult to verify, so for the purpose of *Behind the Masks* she is fictionally employed at the Palace, which according to the previously referenced "Map of Bodie . . ." was located on Bonanza Street.

Ling Loi Wing is fictional, and the story of miners wanting to kiss babies is borrowed from Mark Twain. Sam Chung was an actual person, and was famously and successfully defended by Patrick Reddy in a murder trial (the series of three trials mentioned in the story actually took place in 1881). Judy Yung's *Chinese Women of America: A Pictorial History*, University of Washington Press, 1986, lucidly assembles a great deal of insight and information on the pioneering Chinese women in the California mining camps and the extreme hardships they endured. Yung writes, "*Mui jai* were girls who had been sold into domestic service by their poor parents. Their owners were expected to provide them with food and lodging and to find them husbands when they came of age. However, in some cases, they were instead sold to brothels."

Constable Kirgan was a real lawman. Pioche Kelley was an outlaw who was made into a corrupt sheriff for the purpose of this story. The 601 vigilante group did exist, and it evicted numerous people it considered undesirable. Roger D. McGrath documents the rough, wild, violent way of life in *Gunfighters, Highwaymen & Vigilantes: Violence on the Frontier*, University of California Press, 1984.

The Horribles presented costumed performances in Bodie, lampooning its residents. *The*

Ghost Town of Bodie, as Reported in the Newspapers of the Day by Russ and Anne Johnson, Chalfant Press, 1967, offers a lively account of daily life, including the antics of the Horribles at the Fourth of July celebration in 1880.

In 1877, the Standard Consolidated Mining Company was formed and the Bodie Miners' Union was organized. Three years later, when this story takes place, over fifty Bodie mining stocks were listed on the San Francisco Stock and Exchange Board. The population at this time was between 6,000 and 10,000. The next year, Bodie's great boom leveled off and its decline began.

Fires have been devastating throughout Bodie's history. Sixty-four buildings were lost in 1892, and in 1932 most of the town was destroyed by fire.

In 1942 the U.S. government halted all gold mining because of the second World War. That removed the main reason for the town's existence, and nearly everyone left.

Bodie State Historic Park opened to the public in 1962. The Park is open year-round but in winter it is accessible only by skis, snowshoes, or snow-mobiles. For more information, visit www.parks.ca.gov.

An overview of Bodie, California, from around 1880. The fires of 1892 and 1932 both contributed to destroying much of the town. However, there are some buildings still standing today. Those left are in what is called a "state of arrested decay."

The Occidental Hotel was located along Main Street (seen here to the right of City Market). Unfortunately, the hotel is no longer standing.

A view down one of Bodie's streets in 1877.

The Bodie Standard Mill in 1879. Although it burned down in 1899, it was rebuilt within a year. The Standard still stands today; however, it's no longer a working mill.

Bodie residents outside a cabin.

Stage coaches lined up outside the Grand Central Hotel in Bodie, California.

A Bodie couple in 1879.

A group of Standard miners with an ore train. Once mined, the ore went to the Standard Mill to be processed.

C. R. Wedertz's Bodie Meat Market in the early 1900s.

Anti-Chinese sentiments were common in the second half of the 1800s, especially in California. Many feared that Chinese immigrants were being hired for available jobs because they would work for cheaper wages. The above engraving depicts Denis Kearney inciting an anti-Chinese mob in San Francisco in the late 1800s. Kearney was a California politician known for his public anti-Chinese views. Extreme racism, including violent attacks and riots such as these, took place throughout the West during this time and led to the Chinese Exclusion Act of 1882, a shameful chapter in U.S. history.

Residents gathered together for a holiday celebration. Because no trees grew in Bodie, they were hauled into town from outlying areas and lashed to buildings or fences for decorations during holiday celebrations such as this one.

A modern map of the United States showing Bodie, California.

Mask Making circa 1880

Cut loose-weave cotton muslin into ¾" x 3" strips. Cut some of the strips in half lengthwise and some in half crosswise so you have three sizes of strips to use, as needed.

Fixative:

If you are going to dye the fabric, use this fixative: Mix 1 part vinegar with 4 parts water in a pot. Add fabric and simmer for 1 hour. Rinse in cool water and squeeze out excess.

Yellow Dye Bath:

Put 1 cup firmly packed dry onion skins in pot and cover with water by ½". Bring to a boil and simmer 1 hour. Strain onion skins. Put muslin fabric strips in dye bath. Simmer, covered, until color you desire is achieved. You can turn off the heat under the water and let it sit as long as overnight. The longer you leave the fabric in the dye, the darker the color. Note that the color will lighten as the fabric dries. Rinse in cool water and lay in a single layer on a towel to dry.

Paste:

You'll need 2½ ounces of wheat flour (before weighing, we strained the whole wheat flour to remove the big pieces of bran). From a 1-pint measure of water, add water to flour until you have a smooth paste with no lumps. This will not use all the water. Put the remaining water in a pot and bring to a boil. Pour the boiling water into the mixed flour and water, stirring all the while. Put the mixture back in the pot and boil 5 minutes. When it cools, it will be a thick paste. Thin with water to a pancake batter consistency.

Mask:

It works best to do this project with a partner. Coat one face with a light layer of Vaseline to protect the skin. Dip a strip of fabric in the paste and run it between two fingers to remove most of the excess paste (and to evenly distribute the paste). Lay strips on the face in overlapping fashion, leaving eyeholes, going over the nose but not nostrils, and leaving an opening for the mouth. Exact openings can be evened out with scissors when the mask is dry. Sit in the sun or a warm place to dry. (Twenty-first-century people can also use a blow dryer, on low heat, to hurry things along.) When mostly dry, begin to pry the mask off using a small butter knife (rounded top, not sharp). Loosen all the edges and then begin to prod deeper, until you can release the whole mask. The inside will still be damp. Be careful when turning it upside down to keep the nose, forehead, and cheek shapes supported.

Once the mask is thoroughly dry (at least overnight) you can add a another layer of fabric strips. You don't need to use your partner's face again (although that is ideal). You may be able to simulate it with a gourd or upside-down oval bowl.

When your mask is completed and very dry, use small scissors to even the eyeholes and trim the exterior edges.

Use an awl or nail to punch holes in both sides of the mask, even with the eyeholes.

Knot two 18″ pieces of ribbon. Feed an unknotted end through each of the holes from the front to the back.

> — *By the author's sister, niece, and great-niece: Georgia Chun, and Erin and Christen Miskey*

From the Author

I first visited the ghost town of Bodie during a road trip with my husband a dozen years ago. The town, a National Historic Site and a California State Historic Park, is northeast of Yosemite near the Nevada border. It is maintained in a state of "arrested decay," meaning repairs are made to keep buildings upright but there is no attempt to restore them. The interiors remain exactly as they were, with furnishings and goods and peeling wallpaper. I walked the dusty streets and peered into windows and did not feel as if I was on a movie studio lot or in an amusement park. I got a vivid sense of the real people who had lived there: the riches and work, violence and hardship, and the everyday struggles that defined their existence.

After writing a trilogy of novels (*The Higher Power of Lucky*, *Lucky Breaks*, and *Lucky for Good*) about a contemporary girl growing up in a fictional impoverished *former* mining town of the Eastern Sierra, I wondered what it would have been like to come of age in the same region back when the mining towns were booming. I learned that people mostly made their own medicines and cosmetics, soaps and ointments. Girls and women, with the women's rights movements still many years in the future, were subject to the will of fathers, husbands, and sons. Victorian mores dictated rigid and (compared with those of today) constraining standards of dress and behavior. The daily work was immense. Immigrants and people of parallel cultures were subject to racism and inequality under the law. Miners worked twelve-hour shifts and six-day weeks. Saloons were open twenty-four hours a day. The California Red Light Abatement Act that declared brothels public nuisances was not passed until 1913. So in 1880, though mainstream society did not approve of this way of life, it was legal for women to work in brothels.

The more I read about Bodie and some of the actual people who lived there in 1880, the height of its gold-rush boom, the more I wanted to *imagine* the story of an ordinary girl, her family and friends, against the backdrop of that extraordinary time and place.

I was especially inspired by material that was written in the 1870s and 1880s, which provided tremendous access to how people thought, what they ate, the way they lived. I relied heavily on *Practical Housekeeping, A Careful Compilation of Tried and Approved Recipes*, Buckeye, 1881, for insight into Angie's daily life: The recipes for freckle removal, hair tonic, moth treatment, protective ointment for the face, gray hair preventative, and pigs feet souse, as well as directions for cleaning a woodstove, are taken from its pages. Similarly, *Let Them Speak for Themselves: Women in the American West 1849–1900*, edited by Christiane Fischer, Shoe String Press/Archon, 1977, shows how western life was experienced by women through their uncensored letters, diaries, reminiscences, and journals. I paged through the handwritten ledgers of the 1880 U.S. Census for Bodie, scanning the columns: occupations ("house keeper," "gentleman," "miner," "show man," "cook," "gambler"), ages, places of birth, roles in household — thrilled by the realization that I was viewing a vivid snapshot, taken at the time, of the people who lived there. Another rich source of primary material, *The Saga of Inyo County, California*, Taylor, 1977, provided informal, personal histories that made me feel steeped in the times and able to imagine a life like Angie's in the neighboring county of Mono.

I discovered that Bodieites loved their festive masquerade balls. Masks were also worn by highwaymen and robbers, by vigilantes, by actors for theatrical performances, and at the end, death masks served as a way to commemorate loved ones. Masks hide our secrets, our fears, our regrets, our identity, and our hopes. I came upon a quote by Annaeus Lucanus (often incorrectly attributed to John Dryden, a translator of Latin texts), "Boldness is a mask for fear, however great." To find out if that is true, I peeked behind some of the masks in Bodie and found stories waiting to be told.

Susan Patron is the Newbery Award-winning author of *The Higher Power of Lucky*, among many other books for children, including the Billy Que trilogy of picture books; *Dark Cloud Strong Breeze*; a chapter book, *Maybe Yes, Maybe No, Maybe Maybe*, which was an ALA Notable Book; and two sequels to *The Higher Power of Lucky*: *Lucky Breaks* and *Lucky for Good*. She was a children's librarian at the Los Angeles Public Library for thirty-five years before retiring in 2007, and currently lives in Los Angeles.

Acknowledgments

In striving to capture historical details as authentically and seamlessly as possible, I owe a great debt, for their unstinting help and expert advice (although any errors are my own), to the following: Robert P. Palazzo, knowledgeable as to weapons of the period, was generously receptive to my questions. He has written extensively about the Reddy brothers, Ned and Patrick, and also responded to my queries about them. Terri Lynn Geissinger, Business Manager of the Bodie Foundation, met me in the Bodie Museum and kindly answered questions after my husband and I had explored the town in the fall of 2010. Grateful thanks to Dr. Joseph L. Dautremont, DDS, for his vivid description of late nineteenth-century dental practices and for reviewing that section of the manuscript. I'm privileged that Dr. Judy Yung, professor emerita in American Studies at the University of California, Santa Cruz, an authority on the history of the Chinese and Chinese Americans in the West, read this book in manuscript form and responded with insightful and useful suggestions and comments. Her time and expertise are hugely appreciated.

An enormous boon to me in writing the mask-making

scene were the careful notes and photographs provided by an intrepid three-generation team of Georgia Chun, Erin Miskey, and Christen Miskey, who re-created the process using period ingredients and techniques. Patricia Leavengood (with her insight and ideas on the subject of masks) and Georgia Chun boosted morale as always.

Many thanks to Lisa Sandell and Jody Corbett for their kindness, enthusiasm, and editorial expertise. Thanks again to Susan Cohen and to Kirby Larson for advice and encouragement.

Much appreciation to Lloyd Woolever for generously lending me unique materials from his collection.

Theresa Nelson redefines friendship and bigheartedness. She helped me see ways to make this a better book than it otherwise would have been. Thanks, too, to our cohort Virginia Walter.

René Patron made my writing of this book (as with all else in life) fun, rewarding, and possible.

Grateful acknowledgment is made for permission to use the following:
Cover portrait by Tim O'Brien.
Cover background: courtesy of California State Parks, 2011, West Sacramento, California.
Page 284: Overview of Bodie, California, 1880, courtesy of Mono County Historical Society, Bridgeport, California.
Page 285 (top): Site of the Occidental Hotel, Bodie, California, ibid.

Page 285 (bottom): View down one of Bodie's streets, 1877, ibid.

Page 286 (top): Bodie Standard Mill, 1879, ibid.

Page 286 (bottom): Bodie cabin, ibid.

Page 287 (top): Grand Central Hotel, courtesy of California State Parks, 2011, West Sacramento, California.

Page 287 (bottom): Bodie couple, 1879, courtesy of Mono County Historical Society, Bridgeport, California.

Page 288 (top): Standard Mill miners with ore train, 1902, ibid.

Page 288 (bottom): Wedertz Meat Market, early 1900s, ibid.

Page 289: Engraving of anti-Chinese riots, North Wind Picture Archives, Alfred, Maine.

Page 290 (top): Holiday celebration, 1800s, courtesy of Mono County Historical Society, Bridgeport, California.

Page 290 (bottom): Map by Jim McMahon.

Other books in the Dear America serie

DEAR AMERICA

The Diary of Emma Simpson

When Will This
Cruel War Be Over?
Gordonsville, Virginia, 1864

BARRY DENENBERG

DEAR AMERICA

The Diary of Deliverance Trembley,
Witness to the Salem Witch Trials

I Walk in Dread
Massachusetts Bay Colony, 1691

LISA ROWE FRAUSTINO

DEAR AMERICA

The Diary of Hattie Campbell

Across the Wide and
Lonesome Prairie
The Oregon Trail, 1847

KRISTIANA GREGORY

DEAR AMERICA

The Diary of Abigail Jane Stewart

The Winter of
Red Snow
Valley Forge, Pennsylvania, 1777

KRISTIANA GREGORY

DEAR AMERICA

The Second Diary
of Abigail Jane Stewart

Cannons at Dawn
Valley Forge, Pennsylvania, 1779

KRISTIANA GREGORY

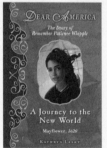

DEAR AMERICA

The Diary of Patsy, a Freed Girl

I Thought My Soul Would
Rise and Fly
Mars Bluff, South Carolina, 1865

JOYCE HANSEN

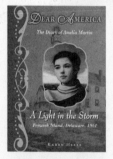

DEAR AMERICA

The Diary of Amelia Martin

A Light in the Storm
Fenwick Island, Delaware, 1861

KAREN HESSE

DEAR AMERICA

The Diary of Piper Davis

The Fences Between Us
Seattle, Washington, 1941

KIRBY LARSON

DEAR AMERICA

The Diary of
Remember Patience Whipple

A Journey to the
New World
Mayflower, 1620

KATHRYN LASKY

DEAR AMERICA

The Diary of Lydia Amelia

LIKE THE
WILLOW TRE
Portland, Maine, 1918

LOIS LOWRY

DEAR AMERICA

The Diary of Clotee, a Slave Girl

A Picture of
Freedom
Belmont Plantation, Virginia, 1859

PATRICIA C. MCKISSACK

DEAR AMERICA

The Diary of Catharine Carey Logan

Standing in the Light
Delaware Valley, Pennsylvania, 1763

MARY POPE OSBORNE

DEAR AMERICA

The Diary of Dawnie Rae Johnson

With the Might
of Angels
Hadley, Virginia, 1954

ANDREA DAVIS PINKNEY

DEAR AMERICA

The Diary of Margaret Ann

Voyage on
the Great Titan
RMS Titanic, 1912

ELLEN EMERSON WH